FLYING U RANCH

By

B. M. Bower

Other Works
by
B.M Bower

Cabin Fever
Casey Ryan
Chip, of the Flying U
Cow-Country
The Flying U Ranch
The Flying U's Last Stand
Good Indian
The Gringos
The Happy Family
The Heritage of the Sioux
Her Prairie Knight
Jean of the Lazy A
Lonesome Land
The Lonesome Trail and Other Stories
The Long Shadow
The Lookout Man
The Lure of the Dim Trails
The Phantom Herd
The Quirt
The Range Dwellers
Rowdy of the Cross L
Skyrider
Starr, of the Desert
The Thunder Bird
The Trail of the White Mule
The Uphill Climb

CHAPTER I. The Coming of a Native Son

The Happy Family, waiting for the Sunday supper call, were grouped around the open door of the bunk-house, gossiping idly of things purely local, when the Old Man returned from the Stock Association at Helena; beside him on the buggy seat sat a stranger. The Old Man pulled up at the bunk-house, the stranger sprang out over the wheel with the agility which bespoke youthful muscles, and the Old Man introduced him with a quirk of the lips:

"This is Mr. Mig-u-ell Rapponi, boys—a peeler straight from the Golden Gate. Throw out your war-bag and make yourself to home, Mig-u-ell; some of the boys'll show you where to bed down."

The Old Man drove on to the house with his own luggage, and Happy Jack followed to take charge of the team; but the remainder of the Happy Family unobtrusively took the measure of the foreign element. From his black-and-white horsehair hatband, with tassels that swept to the very edge of his gray hatbrim, to the crimson silk neckerchief draped over the pale blue bosom of his shirt; from the beautifully stamped leather cuffs, down to the exaggerated height of his tan boot-heels, their critical eyes swept in swift, appraising glances; and unanimous disapproval was the result. The Happy Family had themselves an eye to picturesque garb upon occasion, but this passed even Pink's love of display.

"He's some gaudy to look at," Irish murmured under his breath to Cal Emmett.

"All he lacks is a spot-light and a brass band," Cal returned, in much the same tone with which a woman remarks upon a last season's hat on the head of a rival.

Miguel was not embarrassed by the inspection. He was tall, straight, and swarthily handsome, and he stood with the complacence of a stage favorite waiting for the applause to cease so that he might speak his first lines; and, while he waited, he sifted tobacco into a cigarette paper

3

daintily, with his little finger extended. There was a ring upon that finger; a ring with a moonstone setting as large and round as the eye of a startled cat, and the Happy Family caught the pale gleam of it and drew a long breath. He lighted a match nonchalantly, by the artfully simple method of pinching the head of it with his fingernails, leaned negligently against the wall of the bunk-house, and regarded the group incuriously while he smoked.

"Any pretty girls up this way?" he inquired languidly, after a moment, fanning a thin smoke-cloud from before his face while he spoke.

The Happy Family went prickly hot. The girls in that neighborhood were held in esteem, and there was that in his tone which gave offense.

"Sure, there's pretty girls here!" Big Medicine bellowed unexpectedly, close beside him. "We're all of us engaged to `em, by cripes!"

Miguel shot an oblique glance at Big Medicine, examined the end of his cigarette, and gave a lift of shoulder, which might mean anything or nothing, and so was irritating to a degree. He did not pursue the subject further, and so several belated retorts were left tickling futilely the tongues of the Happy Family—which does not make for amiability.

To a man they liked him little, in spite of their easy friendliness with mankind in general. At supper they talked with him perfunctorily, and covertly sneered because he sprinkled his food liberally with cayenne and his speech with Spanish words pronounced with soft, slurred vowels that made them sound unfamiliar, and against which his English contrasted sharply with its crisp, American enunciation. He met their infrequent glances with the cool stare of absolute indifference to their opinion of him, and their perfunctory civility with introspective calm.

The next morning, when there was riding to be done, and Miguel appeared at the last moment in his working clothes, even Weary, the sunny-hearted, had an unmistakable curl of his lip after the first glance.

Miguel wore the hatband, the crimson kerchief tied loosely with the point draped over his chest, the stamped leather cuffs and the tan boots with the highest heels ever built by the cobbler craft. Also, the lower half of him was incased in chaps the like of which had never before been brought into Flying U coulee. Black Angora chaps they were; long-haired, crinkly to the very hide, with three white, diamond-shaped patches running down each leg of them, and with the leather waistband stamped elaborately to match the cuffs. The bands of his spurs were two inches wide and inlaid to the edge with beaten silver, and each concho was engraved to represent a large, wild rose, with a golden center. A dollar laid upon the rowels would have left a fringe of prongs all around.

He bent over his sacked riding outfit, and undid it, revealing a wonderful saddle of stamped leather inlaid on skirt and cantle with more beaten silver. He straightened the skirts, carefully ignoring the glances thrown in his direction, and swore softly to himself when he discovered where the leather had been scratched through the canvas wrappings and the end of the silver scroll ripped up. He drew out his bridle and shook it into shape, and the silver mountings and the reins of braided leather with horsehair tassels made Happy Jack's eyes greedy with desire. His blanket was a scarlet Navajo, and his rope a rawhide lariat.

Altogether, his splendor when he was mounted so disturbed the fine mental poise of the Happy Family that they left him jingling richly off by himself, while they rode closely grouped and discussed him acrimoniously.

"By gosh, a man might do worse than locate that Native Son for a silver mine," Cal began, eyeing the interloper scornfully. "It's plumb wicked to ride around with all that wealth and fussy stuff. He must 'a' robbed a bank and put the money all into a riding outfit."

"By golly, he looks to me like a pair uh trays when he comes bow-leggin' along with them white diamonds on his legs," Slim stated solemnly.

"And I'll gamble that's a spot higher than he stacks up in the cow game," Pink observed with the pessimism which matrimony had given him. "You mind him asking about bad horses, last night? That Lizzie-boy never saw a bad horse; they don't grow 'em where he come from. What they don't know about riding they make up for with a swell rig—"

"And, oh, mamma! It sure is a swell rig!" Weary paid generous tribute. "Only I will say old Banjo reminds me of an Irish cook rigged out in silk and diamonds. That outfit on Glory, now—" He sighed enviously.

"Well, I've gone up against a few real ones in my long and varied career," Irish remarked reminiscently, "and I've noticed that a hoss never has any respect or admiration for a swell rig. When he gets real busy it ain't the silver filigree stuff that's going to help you hold connections with your saddle, and a silver-mounted bridle-bit ain't a darned bit better than a plain one."

"Just take a look at him!" cried Pink, with intense disgust. "Ambling off there, so the sun can strike all that silver and bounce back in our eyes. And that braided lariat—I'd sure love to see the pieces if he ever tries to anchor anything bigger than a yearling!"

"Why, you don't think for a minute he could ever get out and rope anything, do yuh?" Irish laughed. "That there Native Son throws on a-w-l-together too much dog to really get out and do anything."

"Aw," fleered Happy Jack, "he ain't any Natiff Son. He's a dago!"

"He's got the earmarks uh both," Big Medicine stated authoritatively. "I know 'em, by cripes, and I know their ways." He jerked his thumb toward the dazzling Miguel. "I can tell yuh the kinda cow-puncher he is; I've saw 'em workin' at it. Haw-haw-haw! They'll start out to move ten or a dozen head uh tame old cows from one field to another, and there'll be six or eight fellers, rigged up like this here tray-spot, ridin' along, important as hell, drivin' them few cows down a lane, with peach trees on both sides, by cripes, jingling their big, silver spurs, all wearin' fancy chaps to ride four or five miles down the road. Honest to grandma, they call that punchin' cows! Oh, he's a Native Son, all right. I've saw lots of 'em, only I never saw one so far away from the Promised Land before. That there looks queer to me. Natiff Sons—the real ones, like him—are as scarce outside Calyforny as buffalo are right here in this coulee."

"That's the way they do it, all right," Irish agreed. "And then they'll have a 'rodeo'—"

"Haw-haw-haw!" Big Medicine interrupted, and took up the tale, which might have been entitled "Some Cowpunching I Have Seen."

"They have them rodeos on a Sunday, mostly, and they invite everybody to it, like it was a picnic. And there'll be two or three fellers to every calf, all lit up, like Mig-u-ell, over there, in chaps and silver fixin's, fussin' around on horseback in a corral, and every feller trying to pile his rope on the same calf, by cripes! They stretch 'em out with two ropes—calves, remember! Little, weenty fellers you could pack under one arm! Yuh can't blame 'em much. They never have more'n thirty or forty head to brand at a time, and they never git more'n a taste uh real work. So they make the most uh what they git, and go in heavy on fancy outfits. And this here silver-mounted fellow thinks he's a real cowpuncher, by cripes!"

The Happy Family laughed at the idea; laughed so loud that Miguel left his lonely splendor and swung over to them, ostensibly to borrow a match.

"What's the joke?" he inquired languidly, his chin thrust out and his eyes upon the match blazing at the end of his cigarette.

The Happy Family hesitated and glanced at one another. Then Cal spoke truthfully.

"You're it," he said bluntly, with a secret desire to test the temper of this dark-skinned son of the West.

Miguel darted one of his swift glances at Cal, blew out his match and threw it away.

"Oh, how funny. Ha-ha." His voice was soft and absolutely expressionless, his face blank of any emotion whatever. He merely spoke the words as a machine might have done.

If he had been one of them, the Happy Family would have laughed at the whimsical humor of it. As it was, they repressed the impulse, though Weary warmed toward him slightly.

"Don't you believe anything this innocent-eyed gazabo tells you, Mr. Rapponi," he warned amiably. "He's known to be a liar."

"That's funny, too. Ha-ha some more." Miguel permitted a thin ribbon of smoke to slide from between his lips, and gazed off to the crinkled line of hills.

"Sure, it is—now you mention it," Weary agreed after a perceptible pause.

"How fortunate that I brought the humor to your attention," drawled Miguel, in the same expressionless tone, much as if he were reciting a text.

"Virtue is its own penalty," paraphrased Pink, not stopping to see whether the statement applied to the subject.

"Haw-haw-haw!" roared Big Medicine, quite as irrelevantly.

"He-he-he," supplemented the silver-trimmed one.

Big Medicine stopped laughing suddenly, reined his horse close to the other, and stared at him challengingly, with his pale, protruding eyes, while the Happy Family glanced meaningly at one another. Big Medicine was quite as unsafe as he looked, at that moment, and they wondered if the offender realized his precarious situation.

Miguel smoked with the infinite leisure which is a fine art when it is not born of genuine abstraction, and none could decide whether he was aware of the unfriendly proximity of Big Medicine. Weary was just on the point of saying something to relieve the tension, when Miguel blew the ash gently from his cigarette and spoke lazily.

"Parrots are so common, out on the Coast, that they use them in cheap restaurants for stew. I've often heard them gabbling together in the kettle."

The statement was so ambiguous that the Happy Family glanced at him doubtfully. Big Medicine's stare became more curious than hostile, and he permitted his horse to lag a length. It is difficult to fight absolute passivity. Then Slim, who ever tramped solidly over the flowers of sarcasm, blurted one of his unexpected retorts.

"I was just wonderin', by golly, where yuh learnt to talk!"

Miguel turned his velvet eyes sleepily toward the speaker. "From the boarders who ate those parrots, amigo," he smiled serenely.

At this, Slim—once justly accused by Irish of being a "single-shot" when it came to repartee—turned purple and dumb. The Happy Family, forswearing loyalty in their enjoyment of his discomfiture, grinned and left to Miguel the barren triumph of the last word.

He did not gain in popularity as the days passed. They tilted noses at his beautiful riding gear, and would have died rather than speak of it in his presence. They never gossiped with him of horses or men or the lands he knew. They were ready to snub him at a moment's notice—and it did not lessen their dislike of him that he failed to yield them an opportunity. It is to be hoped that he found his thoughts sufficient entertainment, since he was left to them as much as is humanly possible when half a dozen men eat and sleep and work together. It annoyed them exceedingly that Miguel did not seem to know that they held him at a distance; they objected to his manner of smoking cigarettes and staring off at the skyline as if he were alone and content with his dreams. When he did talk they listened with an air of weary tolerance. When he did not talk they ignored his presence, and when he was absent they criticized him mercilessly.

They let him ride unwarned into an adobe patch one day—at least, Big Medicine, Pink, Cal Emmett and Irish did, for they were with him—and laughed surreptitiously together while he wallowed there and came out afoot, his horse floundering behind him, mud to the ears, both of them.

"Pretty soft going, along there, ain't it?" Pink commiserated deceitfully.

"It is, kinda," Miguel responded evenly, scraping the adobe off Banjo with a flat rock. And the subject was closed.

"Well, it's some relief to the eyes to have the shine taken off him, anyway," Pink observed a little guiltily afterward.

"I betche he ain't goin' to forget that, though," Happy Jack warned when he saw the caked mud on Miguel's Angora chaps and silver spurs, and the condition of his saddle. "Yuh better watch out and not turn your backs on him in the dark, none uh you guys. I betche he packs a knife. Them kind always does."

"Haw-haw-haw!" bellowed Big Medicine uproariously. "I'd love to see him git out an' try to use it, by cripes!"

"I wish Andy was here," Pink sighed. "Andy'd take the starch outa him, all right."

"Wouldn't he be pickings for old Andy, though? Gee!" Cal looked around at them, with his wide, baby-blue eyes, and laughed. "Let's kinda jolly him along, boys, till Andy gets back. It sure would be great to watch 'em. I'll bet he can jar the eternal calm outa that Native Son. That's what grinds me worse than his throwin' on so much dog; he's so blamed satisfied with himself! You snub him, and he looks at yuh as if you was his hired man—and then forgets all about yuh. He come outa that 'doby like he'd been swimmin' a river on a bet, and had made good and was a hee-ro right before the ladies. Kinda 'Oh, that's nothing to what I could do if it was worth while,' way he had with him."

"It wouldn't matter so much if he wasn't all front," Pink complained. "You'll notice that's always the way, though. The fellow all fussed up with silver and braided leather can't get out and do anything. I remember up on Milk river—" Pink trailed off into absorbing reminiscence, which, however, is too lengthy to repeat here.

"Say, Mig-u-ell's down at the stable, sweatin from every pore trying to get his saddle clean, by golly!" Slim reported cheerfully, just as Pink was relighting the cigarette which had gone out during the big scene of his story. "He was cussin' in Spanish, when I walked up to him—but he shut up when he seen me and got that peaceful look uh hisn on his face. I wonder, by golly—"

"Oh, shut up and go awn," Irish commanded bluntly, and looked at Pink. "Did he call it off, then? Or did you have to wade in—"

"Naw; he was like this here Native Son—all front. He could look sudden death, all right; he had black eyes like Mig-u-ell—but all a fellow had to do was go after him, and he'd back up so blamed quick—"

Slim listened that far, saw that he had interrupted a tale evidently more interesting than anything he could say, and went off, muttering to himself.

CHAPTER II. "When Greek Meets Greek"

The next morning, which was Sunday, the machinations of Big Medicine took Pink down to the creek behind the bunk-house. "What's hurtin' yuh?" he asked curiously, when he came to where Big Medicine stood in the fringe of willows, choking between his spasms of mirth.

"Haw-haw-haw!" roared Big Medicine; and, seizing Pink's arm in a gorilla-like grip, he pointed down the bank.

Miguel, seated upon a convenient rock in a sunny spot, was painstakingly combing out the tangled hair of his chaps, which he had washed quite as carefully not long before, as the cake of soap beside him testified.

"Combing—combing—his chaps, by cripes!" Big Medicine gasped, and waggled his finger at the spectacle. "Haw-haw-haw! C-combin'—his—chaps!"

Miguel glanced up at them as impersonally as if they were two cackling hens, rather than derisive humans, then bent his head over a stubborn knot and whistled La Paloma softly while he coaxed out the tangle.

Pink's eyes widened as he looked, but he did not say anything. He backed up the path and went thoughtfully to the corrals, leaving Big Medicine to follow or not, as he chose.

"Combin'—his chaps, by cripes!" came rumbling behind him. Pink turned.

"Say! Don't make so much noise about it," he advised guardedly. "I've got an idea."

"Yuh want to hog-tie it, then," Big Medicine retorted, resentful because Pink seemed not to grasp the full humor of the thing. "Idees sure seems to be skurce in this outfit—or that there lily-uh-the-valley couldn't set and comb no chaps in broad daylight, by cripes; not and get off with it."

"He's an ornament to the Flying U," Pink stated dreamily. "Us boneheads don't appreciate him, is all that ails us. What we ought to do is—help him be as pretty as he wants to be, and—"

11

"Looky here, Little One." Big Medicine hurried his steps until he was close alongside. "I wouldn't give a punched nickel for a four-horse load uh them idees, and that's the truth." He passed Pink and went on ahead, disgust in every line of his square-shouldered figure. "Combin' his chaps, by cripes!" he snorted again, and straightway told the tale profanely to his fellows, who laughed until they were weak and watery-eyed as they listened.

Afterward, because Pink implored them and made a mystery of it, they invited Miguel to take a hand in a long-winded game—rather, a series of games—of seven-up, while his chaps hung to dry upon a willow by the creek bank—or so he believed.

The chaps, however, were up in the white-house kitchen, where were also the reek of scorched hair and the laughing expostulations of the Little Doctor and the boyish titter of Pink and Irish, who were curling laboriously the chaps of Miguel with the curling tongs of the Little Doctor and those of the Countess besides.

"It's a shame, and I just hope Miguel thrashes you both for it," the Little Doctor told them more than once; but she laughed, nevertheless, and showed Pink how to give the twist which made of each lock a corkscrew ringlet. The Countess stopped, with her dishcloth dangling from one red, bony hand, while she looked. "You boys couldn't sleep nights if you didn't pester the life outa somebody," she scolded. "Seems to me I'd friz them diamonds, if I was goin' to be mean enough to do anything."

"You would, eh?" Pink glanced up at her and dimpled. "I'll find you a rich husband to pay for that." He straightway proceeded to friz the diamonds of white.

"Why don't you have a strip of ringlets down each leg, with tight little curls between?" suggested the Little Doctor, not to be outdone by any other woman.

"Correct you are," praised Irish.

"And, remember, you're not heating branding-irons, mister man," she added. "You'll burn all the hair off, if you let the tongs get red-hot. Just so they'll sizzle; I've told you five times already." She picked up the Kid, kissed many times the finger he held up for sympathy—the finger with which he had touched the tongs as Pink was putting them back into the grate of the kitchen stove, and spoke again to ease her conscience. "I think it's awfully mean of you to do it. Miguel ought to thrash you both."

"We're dead willing to let him try, Mrs. Chip. We know it's mean. We're real ashamed of ourselves." Irish tested his tongs as he had been told to do. "But we'd rather be ashamed than good, any old time."

The Little Doctor giggled behind the Kid's tousled curls, and reached out a slim hand once more to give Pink's tongs the expert twist he was trying awkwardly to learn. "I'm sorry for Miguel; he's got lovely eyes, anyway."

"Yes, ain't he?" Pink looked up briefly from his task. "How's your leg, Irish? Mine's done."

"Seems to me I'd make a deep border of them corkscrew curls all around the bottoms, if I was doin' it," said the Countess peevishly, from the kitchen sink. "If I was that dago I'd murder the hull outfit; I never did see a body so hectored in my life—and him not ever ketchin' on. He must be plumb simple-minded."

When the curling was done to the hilarious satisfaction of Irish and Pink, and, while Pink was dancing in them to show them off, another entered with mail from town. And, because the mail-bearer was Andy Green himself, back from a winter's journeyings, Cal, Happy Jack and Slim followed close behind, talking all at once, in their joy at beholding the man they loved well and hated occasionally also. Andy delivered the mail into the hands of the Little Doctor, pinched the Kid's cheek, and said how he had grown good-looking as his mother, almost, spoke a cheerful howdy to the Countess, and turned to shake hands with Pink. It was then that the honest, gray eyes of him widened with amazement.

"Well, by golly!" gasped Slim, goggling at the chaps of Miguel.

"That there Natiff Son'll just about kill yuh for that," warned Happy Jack, as mournfully as he might with laughing. "He'll knife yuh, sure."

Andy, demanding the meaning of it all, learned all about Miguel Rapponi—from the viewpoint of the Happy Family. At least, he learned as much as it was politic to tell in the presence of the Little Doctor; and afterward, while Pink was putting the chaps back upon the willow, where Miguel had left them, he was told that they looked to him, Andy Green, for assistance.

"Oh, gosh! You don't want to depend on me, Pink," Andy expostulated modestly. "I can't think of anything—and, besides, I've reformed. I don't know as it's any compliment to me, by gracious—being told soon as I land that I'm expected to lie to a perfect stranger."

"You come on down to the stable and take a look at his saddle and bridle," urged Cal. "And wait till you see him smoking and looking past you, as if you was an ornery little peak that didn't do nothing but obstruct the scenery. I've seen mean cusses—lots of 'em; and I've seen men that was stuck on themselves. But I never—"

"Come outa that 'doby," Pink interrupted, "mud to his eyebrows, just about. And he knew darned well we headed him in there deliberate. And when I remarks it's soft going, he says: 'It is, kinda,'—just like that." Pink managed to imitate the languid tone of Miguel very well. "Not another word outa him. Didn't even make him mad! He—"

"Tell him about the parrots, Slim," Cal suggested soberly. But Slim only turned purple at the memory, and swore.

"Old Patsy sure has got it in for him," Happy Jack observed. "He asked Patsy if he ever had enchiladas. Patsy won't speak to him no more. He claims Mig-u-ell insulted him. He told Mig-u-ell—"

"Enchiladas are sure fine eating," said Andy. "I took to 'em like a she-bear to honey, down in New Mexico this winter. Your Native Son is solid there, all right."

"Aw, gwan! He ain't solid nowhere but in the head. Maybe you'll love him to death when yuh see him—chances is you will, if you've took to eatin' dago grub."

Andy patted Happy Jack reassuringly on the shoulder. "Don't get excited," he soothed. "I'll put it all over the gentleman, just to show my heart's in the right place. Just this once, though; I've reformed. And I've got to have time to size him up. Where do you keep him when he ain't in the show window?" He swung into step with Pink. "I'll tell you the truth," he confided engagingly. "Any man that'll wear chaps like he's got—even leaving out the extra finish you fellows have given 'em—had ought to be taught a lesson he'll remember. He sure must be a tough proposition, if the whole bunch of yuh have had to give him up. By gracious—"

"We haven't tried," Pink defended. "It kinda looked to us as if he was aiming to make us guy him; so we didn't. We've left him strictly alone. To-day"—he glanced over his shoulder to where the becurled chaps swung comically from the willow branch—"to-day's the first time anybody's made a move. Unless," he added, as an afterthought, "you count yesterday in the 'doby patch—and even then we didn't tell him to ride into it; we just let him do it."

"And kinda herded him over towards it," Cal amended slyly.

"Can he ride?" asked Andy, going straight to the main point, in the mind of a cowpuncher.

"W-e-ell-he hasn't been piled, so far. But then," Pink qualified hastily, "he hasn't topped anything worse than Crow-hop. He ain't hard to ride. Happy Jack could—"

"Aw, I'm gittin' good and sick of hearin' that there tune," Happy growled indignantly. "Why don't you point out Slim as the limit, once in a while?"

"Come on down to the stable, and let's talk it over," Andy suggested, and led the way. "What's his style, anyway? Mouthy, or what?"

With four willing tongues to enlighten him, it would be strange, indeed, if one so acute as Andy Green failed at last to have a very fair mental picture of Miguel. He gazed thoughtfully at his boots, laughed suddenly, and slapped Irish quite painfully upon the back.

"Come on up and introduce me, boys," he said. "We'll make this Native Son so hungry for home—you watch me put it on the gentleman. Only it does seem a shame to do it."

"No, it ain't. If you'd been around him for two weeks, you'd want to kill him just to make him take notice," Irish assured him.

15

"What gets me," Andy mused, "is why you fellows come crying to me for help. I should think the bunch of you ought to be able to handle one lone Native Son."

"Aw, you're the biggest liar and faker in the bunch, is why," Happy Jack blurted.

"Oh, I see." Andy hummed a little tune and pushed his hands deep into his pockets, and at the corners of his lips there flickered a smile.

The Native Son sat with his hat tilted slightly back upon his head and a cigarette between his lips, and was reaching lazily for the trick which made the fourth game his, when the group invaded the bunk-house. He looked up indifferently, swept Andy's face and figure with a glance too impersonal to hold even a shade of curiosity, and began rapidly shuffling his cards to count the points he had made.

Andy stopped short, just inside the door, and stared hard at Miguel, who gave no sign. He turned his honest, gray eyes upon Pink and Irish accusingly—whereat they wondered greatly.

"Your deal—if you want to play," drawled Miguel, and shoved his cards toward Big Medicine. But the boys were already uptilting chairs to grasp the quicker the outstretched hand of the prodigal, so that Miguel gathered up the cards, evened their edges mechanically, and deigned another glance at this stranger who was being welcomed so vociferously. Also he sighed a bit—for even a languid-eyed stoic of a Native Son may feel the twinge of loneliness. Andy shook hands all round, swore amiably at Weary, and advanced finally upon Miguel.

"You don't know me from Adam's off ox," he began genially, "but I know you, all right, all right. I hollered my head off with the rest of 'em when you played merry hell in that bull-ring, last Christmas. Also, I was part of your bodyguard when them greasers were trying to tickle you in the ribs with their knives in that dark alley. Shake, old-timer! You done yourself proud, and I'm glad to know yuh!"

Miguel, for the first time in two weeks, permitted himself the luxury of an expressive countenance. He gave Andy Green one quick, grateful look—and a smile, the like of which made the Happy Family quiver inwardly with instinctive sympathy.

"So you were there, too, eh?" Miguel exclaimed softly, and rose to greet him. "And that scrap in the alley—we sure had a hell of a time there for a few minutes, didn't we? Are you that tall fellow who kicked that squint-eyed greaser in the stomach? Muchos gracios, senor! They were piling on me three deep, right then, and I always believed they'd have got me, only for a tall vaquero I couldn't locate afterward." He smiled again that wonderful smile, which lighted the darkness of his eyes as with a flame, and murmured a sentence or two in Spanish.

"Did you get the spurs me and my friends sent you afterward?" asked Andy eagerly. "We heard about the Arizona boys giving you the saddle—and we raked high and low for them spurs. And, by gracious, they were beauts, too—did yuh get 'em?"

"I wear them every day I ride," answered Miguel, a peculiar, caressing note in his voice.

"I didn't know—we heard you had disappeared off the earth. Why—"

Miguel laughed outright. "To fight a bull with bare hands is one thing, amigo," he said. "To take a chance on getting a knife stuck in your back is another. Those Mexicans—they don't love the man who crosses the river and makes of their bull-fights a plaything."

"That's right; only I thought, you being a—"

"Not a Mexican." Miguel's voice sharpened a trifle. "My father was Spanish, yes. My mother"—his eyes flashed briefly at the faces of the gaping Happy Family—"my mother was born in Ireland."

"And that sure makes a hard combination to beat," cried Andy heartily. He looked at the others—at all, that is, save Pink and Irish, who had disappeared. "Well, boys, I never thought I'd come home and find—"

"Miguel Rapponi," supplied the Native Son quickly. "As well forget that other name. And," he added with the shrug which the Happy Family had come to hate, "as well forget the story, also. I am not hungry for the feel of a knife in my back." He smiled again engagingly at Andy Green. It was astonishing how readily that smile had sprung to life with the warmth of a little friendship, and how pleasant it was, withal.

"Just as you say," Andy agreed, not trying to hide his admiration. "I guess nobody's got a better right to holler for silence. But—say, you sure delivered the goods, old boy! You musta read about it, you fellows; about the American puncher that went over the line and rode one of their crack bulls all round the ring, and then—" He stopped and looked apologetically at Miguel, in whose dark eyes there flashed a warning light. "I clean forgot," he confessed impulsively. "This meeting you here unexpectedly, like this, has kinda got me rattled, I guess. But—I never saw yuh before in my life," he declared emphatically. "I don't know a darn thing about—anything that ever happened in an alley in the city of—oh, come on, old-timer; let's talk about the weather, or something safe!"

After that the boys of the Flying U behaved very much as do children who have quarreled foolishly and are trying shamefacedly to re-establish friendly relations without the preliminary indignity of open repentance. They avoided meeting the velvet-eyed glances of Miguel, and at the same time they were plainly anxious to include him in their talk as if that had been their habit from the first. A difficult situation to meet, even with the fine aplomb of the Happy Family to ease the awkwardness.

Later Miguel went unobtrusively down to the creek after his chaps; he did not get them, just then, but he stood for a long time hidden behind the willow-fringe, watching Pink and Irish feverishly combing out certain corkscrew ringlets, and dampening their combs in the creek to facilitate the process of straightening certain patches of rebellious frizzes. Miguel did not laugh aloud, as Big Medicine had done. He stood until he wearied of the sight, then lifted his shoulders in the gesture which may mean anything, smiled and went his way.

Not until dusk did Andy get a private word with him. When he did find him alone, he pumped Miguel's hand up and down and afterward clutched at the manger for support, and came near strangling. Miguel leaned beside him and smiled to himself.

"Good team work, old boy," Andy gasped at length, in a whisper. "Best I ever saw in m'life, impromptu on the spot, like that. I saw you had the makings in you, soon as I caught your eye. And the whole, blame bunch fell for it—woo-oof!" He laid his face down again upon his folded arms and shook in all the long length of him.

"They had it coming," said Miguel softly, with a peculiar relish. "Two whole weeks, and never a friendly word from one of them—oh, hell!"

"I know—I heard it all, soon as I hit the ranch," Andy replied weakly, standing up and wiping his eyes. "I just thought I'd learn 'em a lesson—and the way you played up—say, my hat's off to you, all right!"

"One learns to seize opportunities without stuttering," Miguel observed calmly—and a queer look came into his eyes as they rested upon the face of Andy. "And, if the chance comes, I'll do as much for you. By the way, did you see the saddle those Arizona boys sent me? It's over here. It's a pip-pin—almost as fine as the spurs, which I keep in the bunk-house when they're not on my heels. And, if I didn't say so before, I'm sure glad to meet the man that helped me through that alley. That big, fat devil would have landed me, sure, if you hadn't—"

"Ah—what?" Andy leaned and peered into the face of Miguel, his jaw hanging slack. "You don't mean to tell me—it's true?"

"True? Why, I thought you were the fellow—" Miguel faced him steadily. His eyes were frankly puzzled.

"I'll tell you the truth, so help me," Andy said heavily. "I don't know a darned thing about it, only what I read in the papers. I spent the whole winter in Colorado and Wyoming. I was just joshing the boys."

"Oh," said Miguel.

They stood there in the dusk and silence for a space, after which Andy went forth into the night to meditate upon this thing. Miguel stood and looked after him.

"He's the real goods when it comes to lying—but there are others," he said aloud, and smiled a peculiar smile. But for all that he felt that he was going to like Andy very much indeed. And, since the Happy Family had shown a disposition to make him one of themselves, he knew that he was going to become quite as foolishly attached to the Flying U as was even Slim, confessedly the most rabid of partisans.

In this wise did Miguel Rapponi, then, become a member of Jim Whitmore's Happy Family, and play his part in the events which followed his adoption.

CHAPTER III. Bad News

Andy Green, that honest-eyed young man whom everyone loved, but whom not a man believed save when he was indulging his love for more or less fantastic flights of the imagination, pulled up on the brow of Flying U coulee and stared somberly at the picture spread below him. On the porch of the White House the hammock swung gently under the weight of the Little Doctor, who pushed her shipper-toe mechanically against a post support at regular intervals while she read.

On the steps the Kid was crawling laboriously upward, only to descend again quite as laboriously when he attained the top. One of the boys was just emerging from the blacksmith shop; from the build of him Andy knew it must be either Weary or Irish, though it would take a much closer observation, and some familiarity with the two to identify the man more exactly. In the corral were a swirl of horses and an overhanging cloud of dust, with two or three figures discernible in the midst, and away in the little pasture two other figures were galloping after a fleeing dozen of horses. While he looked, old Patsy came out of the messhouse, and went, with flapping flour-sack apron, to the woodpile.

Peaceful it was, and home-like and contentedly prosperous; a little world tucked away in its hills, with its own little triumphs and defeats, its own heartaches and rejoicings; a lucky little world, because its triumphs had been satisfying, its defeats small, its heartaches brief, and its rejoicings untainted with harassment or guilt. Yet Andy stared down upon it with a frown; and, when he twitched the reins and began the descent, he sighed impatiently.

Past the stable he rode with scarcely a glance toward Weary, who shouted a casual "Hello" at him from the corral; through the big gate and up the trail to the White House, and straight to the porch, where the Little Doctor flipped a leaf of her magazine and glanced at him with a smile, and the Kid turned his plump body upon the middle step and wrinkled his nose in a smile of recognition, while he threw out an arm in welcome, and made a wobbling effort to get upon his feet.

Andy smiled at the Kid, but his smile did not reach his eyes, and faded almost immediately. He glanced at the Little Doctor, sent his horse past the steps and the Kid, and close to the railing, so that he could lean and toss the mail into the Little Doctor's lap. There was a yellow envelope among the letters, and her fingers singled it out curiously. Andy folded his hands upon the saddle-horn and watched her frankly.

"Must be from J. G.," guessed the Little Doctor, inserting a slim finger under the badly sealed flap. "I've been wondering if he wasn't going to send some word—he's been gone a week—Baby! He's right between your horse's legs, Andy! Oh-h—baby boy, what won't you do next?" She scattered letters and papers from her lap and flew to the rescue. "Will he kick, Andy? You little ruffian." She held out her arms coaxingly from the top of the steps, and her face, Andy saw when he looked at her, had lost some of its color.

"The horse is quiet enough," he reassured her. "But at the same time I wouldn't hand him out as a plaything for a kid." He leaned cautiously and peered backward.

"Oh—did you ever see such a child! Come to mother, Baby!" Her voice was becoming strained.

The Kid, wrinkling his nose, and jabbering unintelligibly at her, so that four tiny teeth showed in his pink mouth, moved farther backward, and sat down violently under the horse's sweat-roughened belly. He wriggled round so that he faced forward, reached out gleefully, caught the front fetlocks, and cried "Dup!" while he pulled. The Little Doctor turned white.

"He's all right," soothed Andy, and, leaning with a twist of his slim body, caught the Kid firmly by the back of his pink dress, and lifted him clear of danger. He came up with a red face, tossed the Kid into the eager arms of the Little Doctor, and soothed his horse with soft words and a series of little slaps upon the neck. He was breathing unevenly, because the Kid had really been in rather a ticklish position; but the Little Doctor had her face hidden on the baby's neck and did not see.

"Where's Chip?" Andy turned to ride back to the stable, glancing toward the telegram lying on the floor of the porch; and from it his eyes went to the young woman trying to laugh away her trembling while she scolded adoringly her adventurous man-child. He was about to speak again, but thought better of it, and sighed.

"Down at the stables somewhere—I don't know, really; the boys can tell you. Mother's baby mustn't touch the naughty horses. Naughty horses hurt mother's baby! Make him cry!"

Andy gave her a long look, which had in it much pity, and rode away. He knew what was in that telegram, for the agent had told him when he hunted him up at Rusty Brown's and gave it to him; and the horse of Andy bore mute testimony to the speed with which he had brought it to the ranch. Not until he had reached the coulee had he slackened his pace. He decided, after that glance, that he would not remind her that she had not read the telegram; instead, he thought he ought to find Chip immediately and send him to her.

Chip was rummaging after something in the store-house, and, when Andy saw him there, he dismounted and stood blotting out the light from the doorway. Chip looked up, said "Hello" carelessly, and flung an old slicker aside that he might search beneath it. "Back early, aren't you?" he asked, for sake of saying something.

Andy's attitude was not as casual as he would have had it.

"Say, maybe you better go on up to the house," he began diffidently. "I guess your wife wants to see yuh, maybe."

"Just as a good wife should," grinned Chip. "What's the matter? Kid fall off the porch?"

"N-o-o—I brought out a wire from Chicago. It's from a doctor there—some hospital. The—Old Man got hurt. One of them cussed automobiles knocked him down. They want you to come."

Chip had straightened up and was hooking at Andy blankly. "If you're just—"

"Honest," Andy asserted, and flushed a little. "I'll go tell some one to catch up the team—you'll want to make that 11:20, I take it." He added, as Chip went by him hastily, "I had the agent wire for sleeper berths on the 11:20 so—"

"Thanks. Yes, you have the team caught up, Andy." Chip was already well on his way to the house.

Andy waited till he saw the Little Doctor come hurriedly to the end of the porch overlooking the pathway, with the telegram fluttering in her fingers, and then led his horse down through the gate and to the stable. He yanked the saddle off, turned the tired animal into a stall, and went on to the corral, where he leaned elbows on a warped rail and peered through at the turmoil within. Close beside him stood Weary, with his loop dragging behind him, waiting for a chance to throw it over the head of a buckskin three-year-old with black mane and tail.

"Get in here and make a hand, why don't you?" Weary bantered, his eye on the buckskin. "Good chance to make a 'rep' for yourself, Andy. Gawd greased that buckskin—he sure can slide out from under a rope as easy—"

He broke off to flip the hoop dexterously forward, had the reward of seeing the buckskin dodge backward, so that the rope barely flicked him on the nose, and drew in his rope disgustedly. "Come on, Andy—my hands are up in the air; I can't land him—that's the fourth throw."

Andy's interest in the buckskin, however, was scant. His face was sober, his whole attitude one of extreme dejection.

"You got the tummy-ache?" Pink inquired facetiously, moving around so that he got a fair look at his face.

"Naw—his girl's went back on him!" Happy Jack put in, coiling his rope as he came up.

"Oh, shut up!" Andy's voice was sharp with trouble. "Boys, the Old Man's—well, he's most likely dead by this time. I brought out a telegram—"

23

"Go on!" Pink's eyes widened incredulously. "Don't you try that kind of a load, Andy Green, or I'll just about—"

"Oh, you fellows make me sick!" Andy took his elbows off the rail and stood straight. "Dammit, the telegram's up at the house—go and read it yourselves, then!"

The three stared after him doubtfully, fear struggling with the caution born of much experience.

"He don't act, to me, like he was putting up a josh," Weary stated uneasily, after a minute of silence. "Run up to the house and find out, Cadwalloper. The Old Man—oh, good Lord!" The tan on Weary's face took a lighter tinge. "Scoot—it won't take but a minute to find out for sure. Go on, Pink."

"So help me Josephine, I'll kill that same Andy Green if he's lied about it," Pink declared, while he climbed the fence.

In three minutes he was back, and before he had said a word, his face confirmed the bad news. Their eyes besought him for details, and he gave them jerkily. "Automobile run over him. He ain't dead, but they think—Chip and the Little Doctor are going to catch the night train. You go haze in the team, Happy. And give 'em a feed of oats, Chip said."

Irish and Big Medicine, seeing the three standing soberly together there, and sensing something unusual, came up and heard the news in stunned silence. Andy, forgetting his pique at their first disbelief, came forlornly back and stood with them.

The Old Man—the thing could not be true! To every man of them his presence, conjured by the impending tragedy, was almost a palpable thing. His stocky figure seemed almost to stand in their midst; he looked at them with his whimsical eyes, which had the radiating crows-feet of age, humor and habitual squinting against sun and wind; the bald spot on his head, the wrinkling shirt-collar that seldom knew a tie, the carpet slippers which were his favorite footgear because they were kind to his bunions, his husky voice, good-naturedly complaining, were poignantly real to them at that moment. Then Irish mentally pictured him lying maimed, dying, perhaps, in a far-off hospital among strangers, and swore.

"If he's got to die, it oughta be here, where folks know him and—where he knows—" Irish was not accustomed to giving voice to his deeper feelings, and he blundered awkwardly over it.

"I never did go much on them darned hospitals, anyway," Weary observed gloomily. "He oughta be home, where folks can look after him. Mam-ma! It sure is a fright."

"I betche Chip and the Little Doctor won't get there in time," Happy Jack predicted, with his usual pessimism. "The Old Man's gittin' old—"

"He ain't but fifty-two; yuh call that old, consarn yuh? He's younger right now than you'll be when you're forty."

"Countess is going along, too, so she can ride herd on the Kid," Pink informed then. "I heard the Little Doctor tell her to pack up, and 'never mind if she did have sponge all set!' Countess seemed to think her bread was a darned sight more important than the Old Man. That's the way with women. They'll pass up—"

"Well, by golly, I like to see a woman take some interest in her own affairs," Slim defended. "What they packin' up for, and where they goin'?" Slim had just ridden up to the group in time to overhear Pink's criticism.

They told him the news, and Slim swallowed twice, said "By golly!" quite huskily, and then rode slowly away with his head bowed. He had worked for the Flying U when it was strictly a bachelor outfit, and with the tenacity of slow minds he held J. G. Whitmore, his beloved "Old Man," as but a degree lower than that mysterious power which made the sun to shine—and, if the truth were known, he had accepted him as being quite as eternal. His loyalty adjusted everything to the interests of the Flying U. That the Old Man could die—the possibility stunned him.

They were a sorry company that gathered that night around the long table with its mottled oil-cloth covering and benches polished to a glass-like smoothness with their own vigorous bodies. They did not talk much about the Old Man; indeed, they came no nearer the subject than to ask Weary if he were going to drive the team in to Dry Lake. They did not talk much about anything, for that matter; even the knives and forks seemed to share the general depression of spirits, and failed to give forth the cheerful clatter which was a daily accompaniment of meals in that room.

Old Patsy, he who had cooked for J. G. Whitmore when the Flying U coulee was a wilderness and the brand yet unrecorded and the irons unmade—Patsy lumbered heavily about the room and could not find his dish-cloth when it was squeezed tight in one great, fat hand, and unthinkingly started to fill their coffee cups from the tea-kettle.

"Py cosh, I vould keel der fool vot made her first von of der automobeels, yet!" he exclaimed unexpectedly, after a long silence, and cast his pipe vindictively toward his bunk in one corner.

The Happy Family looked around at him, then understandingly at one another.

"Same here, Patsy," Jack Bates agreed. "What they want of the damned things when the country's full uh good horses gits me."

"So some Yahoo with just sense enough to put goggles on to cover up his fool face can run over folks he ain't good enough to speak to, by cripes!" Big Medicine glared aggressively up and down the table.

Weary got up suddenly and went out, and Slim followed him, though his supper was half-uneaten.

"This goin' to be hard on the Little Doctor—only brother she's got," they heard Happy Jack point out unnecessarily; and Weary, the equable, was guilty of slamming the door so that the whole building shook, by way of demonstrating his dislike of speech upon the subject.

They were a sorry company who waved hands at the Little Doctor and the Kid and the Countess, just when the afterglow of a red sunset was merging into the vague, purple shadows of coming dusk. They stood silent, for the most part, and let them go without the usual facetious advice to "Be good to yourselves," and the hackneyed admonition to Chip to keep out of jail if he could. There must have been something very wistful in their faces, for the Little Doctor smiled bravely down upon then from the buggy seat, and lifted up the Kid for a four-toothed smile and an ecstatic "Bye!" accompanied by a vigorous flopping of hands, which included then all.

"We'll telegraph first thing, boys," the Little Doctor called back, as the rig chucked into the pebbly creek crossing. "We'll keep you posted, and I'll write all the particulars as soon as I can. Don't think the worst—unless you have to. I don't." She smiled again, and waved her hand hastily because of the Kid's contortions; and, though the smile had tears close behind it, though her voice was tremulous in spite of herself, the Happy Family took heart from her courage and waved their hats gravely, and smiled back as best they could.

"There's a lot uh cake you boys might just as well eat up," the Countess called belatedly. "It'll all dry out, if yuh don't—and there ain't no use wastin' it—and there's two lemon pies in the brown cupboard, and what under the shinin' sun—" The wheels bumped violently against a rock, and the Happy Family heard no more.

CHAPTER IV. Some Hopes

On the third day after the Happy Family decided that there should be some word from Chicago; and, since that day was Sunday, they rode in a body to Dry Lake after it. They had not discussed the impending tragedy very much, but they were an exceedingly Unhappy Family, nevertheless; and, since Flying U coulee was but a place of gloom, they were not averse to leaving it behind them for a few hours, and riding where every stick and stone did not remind then of the Old Man.

In Dry Lake was a message, brief but heartening:

"J. G. still alive. Some hopes".

They left the station with lighter spirits after reading that; rode to the hotel, tied their horses to the long hitching pole there and went in. And right there the Happy Family unwittingly became cast for the leading parts in one of those dramas of the West which never is heard of outside the theater in which grim circumstance stages it for a single playing—unless, indeed, the curtain rings down on a tragedy that brings the actors before their district judge for trial. And, as so frequently is the case, the beginning was casual to the point of triviality.

Sary, Ellen, Marg'reet, Sybilly and Jos'phine Denson (spelled in accordance with parental pronunciation) were swinging idly upon the hitching pole, with the self-conscious sang froid of country children come to town. They backed away from the Happy Family's approach, grinned foolishly in response to their careless greeting, and tittered openly at the resplendence of the Native Son, who was wearing his black Angora chaps with the three white diamonds down each leg, the gay horsehair hatband, crimson neckerchief and Mexican spurs with their immense rowels and ornate conchos of hand-beaten silver. Sary, Ellen, Marg'reet, Jos'phine and Sybilly were also resplendent, in their way. Their carroty hair was tied with ribbons quite aggressively new, their freckles shone with maternal scrubbing, and there was a hint of home-made "crochet-lace" beneath each stiffly starched dress.

"Hello, kids," Weary greeted them amiably, with a secret smile over the memory of a time when they had purloined the Little Doctor's pills and had made reluctant acquaintance with a stomach pump. "Where's the circus going to be at?"

"There ain't goin' to be no circus," Sybilly retorted, because she was the forward one of the family. "We're going away; on the train. The next one that comes along. We're going to be on it all night, too; and we'll have to eat on it, too."

"Well, by golly, you'll want something to eat, then!" Slim was feeling abstractedly in his pocket for a coin, for these were the nieces of the Countess, and therefore claimed more than a cursory interest from Slim. "You take this up to the store and see if yuh can't swop it for something good to eat." Because Sary was the smallest of the lot he pressed the dollar into her shrinking, amazed palm.

"Paw's got more money'n that," Sybilly announced proudly. "Paw's got a million dollars. A man bought our ranch and gave him a lot of money. We're rich now. Maybe paw'll buy us a phony-graft. He said maybe he would. And maw's goin' to have a blue silk dress with green onto it. And—"

"Better haze along and buy that grub stake," Slim interrupted the family gift for profuse speech. He had caught the boys grinning, and fancied that they were tracing a likeness between the garrulity of Sybilly and the fluency of her aunt, the Countess. "You don't want that train to go off and leave yuh, by golly."

"Wonder who bought Denson out?" Cal Emmett asked of no one in particular, as the children went strutting off to the store to spend the dollar which little Sary clutched so tightly it seemed as if the goddess of liberty must surely have been imprinted upon her palm.

When they went inside and found Denson himself pompously "setting 'em up to the house," Cal repeated the question in a slightly different form to the man himself.

Denson, while he was ready to impress the beholders with his unaccustomed affluence, became noticeably embarrassed at the inquiry, and edged off into vague generalities.

"I jest nacherlly had to sell when I got m' price," he told the Happy Family in a tone that savored strongly of apology. "I like the country, and I like m' neighbors fine. Never'd ask for better than the Flyin' U has been t' me. I ain't got no kick comin' there. Sorry to hear the Old Man's hurt back East. Mary was real put out at not bein' able to see Louise 'fore she went away"—Louise being the Countess' and Mary Denson's sister—"but soon as I sold I got oneasy like. The feller wanted p'session right away, too, so I told Mary we might as well start b'fore we git outa the notion. I wouldn't uh cared about sellin', maybe, but the kids needs to be in school. They're growin' up in ign'rance out here, and Mary's folks wants us to come back 'n' settle close handy by—they been at us t' sell out and move fer the last five years, now, and I told Mary—"

Even Cal forgot, eventually, that he had asked a question which remained unanswered; what interest he had felt at first was smothered to death beneath that blanket of words, and he eagerly followed the boys out and over to Rusty Brown's place, where Denson, because of an old grudge against Rusty, might be trusted not to follow.

"Mamma!" Weary commented amusedly, when they were crossing the street, "that Denson bunch can sure talk the fastest and longest, and say the least, of any outfit I ever saw."

"Wonder who did buy him out?" Jack Bates queried. "Old ginger-whiskers didn't pass out any facts, yuh notice. He couldn't have got much; his land's mostly gravel and 'doby patches. He's got a water right on Flying U creek, you know—first right, at that, seems to me—and a dandy fine spring in that coulee. Wonder why our outfit didn't buy him out—seeing he wanted to sell so bad?"

"This wantin' to sell is something I never heard of b'fore," Slim said slowly. "To hear him tell it, that ranch uh hisn was worth a dollar an inch, by golly. I don't b'lieve he's been wantin' to sell out. If he had, Mis' Bixby woulda said something about it. She don't know about this here sellin' business, or she'd a said—"

"Yeah, you can most generally bank on the Countess telling all she knows," Cal assented with some sarcasm; at which Slim grunted and turned sulky afterward.

Denson and his affairs they speedily forgot for a time, in the diversion which Rusty Brown's familiar place afforded to young men with unjaded nerves and a zest for the primitive pleasures. Not until mid-afternoon did it occur to them that Flying U coulee was deserted by all save old Patsy, and that there were chores to be done, if all the creatures of the coulee would sleep in comfort that night. Pink, therefore, withdrew his challenge to the bunch, and laid his billiard cue down with a sigh and the remark that all he lacked was time, to have the scalps of every last one of them hanging from his belt. Pink was figurative in his speech, you will understand; and also a bit vainglorious over beating Andy Green and Big Medicine twice in succession.

It occurred to Weary then that a word of cheer to the Old Man and his anxious watchers might not cone amiss. Therefore the Happy Family mounted and rode to the depot to send it, and on the way wrangled over the wording of the message after their usual contentious manner.

"Better tell 'em everything is fine, at this end uh the line," Cal suggested, and was hooted at for a poet.

"Just say," Weary began, when he was interrupted by the discordant clamor from a trainload of sheep that had just pulled in and stopped. "'Maa-aa, Ma-a-aaa,' darn yuh," he shouted derisively, at the peering, plaintive faces, glimpsed between the close-set bars. "Mamma, how I do love sheep!" Whereupon he put spurs to his horse and galloped down to the station to rid his ears of the turbulent wave of protest from the cars.

Naturally it required some time to compose the telegram in a style satisfactory to all parties. Outside, cars banged together, an engine snorted stertorously, and suffocating puffs of coal smoke now and then invaded the waiting-room while the Happy Family were sending that message of cheer to Chicago. If you are curious, the final version of their combined sentiments was not at all spectacular. It said merely:

"Everything fine here. Take good care of the Old Man. How's the Kid stacking up?"

It was signed simply "The Bunch."

"Mary's little lambs are here yet, I see," the Native Son remarked carelessly when they went out. "Enough lambs for all the Marys in the country. How would you like to be Mary?"

"Not for me," Irish declared, and turned his face away from the stench of them.

Others there were who rode the length of the train with faces averted and looks of disdain; cowmen, all of them, they shared the range prejudice, and took no pains to hide it.

The wind blew strong from the east, that day; it whistled through the open, double-decked cars packed with gray, woolly bodies, whose voices were ever raised in strident complaint; and the stench of them smote the unaccustomed nostrils of the Happy Family and put them to disgusted flight up the track and across it to where the air was clean again.

"Honest to grandma, I'd make the poorest kind of a sheepherder," Big Medicine bawled earnestly, when they were well away from the noise and smell of the detested animals. "If I had to herd sheep, by cripes, do you know what I'd do? I'd haze 'em into a coulee and turn loose with a good rifle and plenty uh shells, and call in the coyotes to git a square meal. That's the way I'd herd sheep. It's the only way you can shut 'em up. They just 'baa-aa, baa-aa, baa-aa' from the time they're dropped till somebody kills 'em off. Honest, they blat in their sleep. I've heard 'em."

"When you and the dogs were shooting off coyotes?" asked Andy Green pointedly, and so precipitated dissension which lasted for ten miles.

CHAPTER V. Sheep

Slim rising first from dinner on the next day but one opened the door of the mess-house, and stood there idly picking his teeth before he went about his work. After a minute of listening to the boys "joshing" old Patsy about some gooseberry pies he had baked without sugar, he turned his face outward, threw up his head like a startled bull, and began to sniff.

"Say, I smell sheep, by golly!" he announced in the bellowing tone which was his conversational voice, and sniffed again.

"Oh, that's just a left-over in your system from the dose yuh got in town Sunday," Weary explained soothingly. "I've smelled sheep, and tasted sheep, and dreamed sheep, ever since."

"No, by golly, it's sheep! It ain't no memory. I—I b'hieve I hear 'em, too, by golly." Slim stepped out away from the building and faced suspiciously down the coulee.

"Slim, I never suspected you of imagination before," the Native Son drawled, and loitered out to where Slim stood still sniffing. "I wonder if you're catching it from Andy and me. Don't you think you ought to be vaccinated?"

"That ain't imagination," Pink called out from within. "When anybody claims there's sheep in Flying U coulee, that's straight loco."

"Come on out here and smell 'em yourself, then!" Slim bawled indignantly. "I never seen such an outfit as this is gittin' to be; you fellers don't believe nobody, no more. We ain't all Andy Greens."

Upon hearing this Andy pushed back his chair and strolled outside. He clapped his hand down upon Slim's fat-cushioned shoulder and swayed him gently. "Never mind, Slim; you can't all be famous," he comforted. "Some day, maybe, I'll teach yuh the fine art of lying more convincingly than the ordinary man can tell the truth. It is a fine art; it takes a genius to put it across. Now, the only time anybody doubts my word is when I'm sticking to the truth hike a sand burr to a dog's tail."

From away to the west, borne on the wind which swept steadily down the coulee, came that faint, humming sing-song, which can be made only by a herd of a thousand or more sheep, all blatting in different keys—or by a distant band playing monotonously upon the middle octave of their varied instruments.

"Slim's right, by gracious! It's sheep, sure as yuh live." Andy did not wait for more, but started at a fast walk for the stable and his horse. After him went the Native Son, who had not been with the Flying U long enough to sense the magnitude of the affront, and Slim, who knew to a nicety just what "cowmen" considered the unpardonable sin, and the rest of the Happy Family, who were rather incredulous still.

"Must be some fool herder just crossing the coulee, on the move somewhere," Weary gave as a solution. "Half of 'em don't know a fence when they see it."

As they galloped toward the sound and the smell, they expressed freely their opinion of sheep, the men who owned them, and the lunatics who watched over the blatting things. They were cattlemen to the marrow in their bones, and they gloried in their prejudice against the woolly despoilers of the range.

All these years had the Flying U been immune from the nuisance, save for an occasional trespasser, who was quickly sent about his business. The Flying U range had been kept in the main inviolate from the little, gray vandals, which ate the grass clean to the sod, and trampled with their sharp-pointed hoofs the very roots into lifelessness; which polluted the water-holes and creeks until cattle and horses went thirsty rather than drink; which, in that land of scant rainfall, devastated the range where they fed so that a long-established prairie-dog town was not more barren. What wonder if the men who owned cattle, and those who tended them, hated sheep? So does the farmer dread an invasion of grasshoppers.

A mile down the coulee they came upon the band with two herders and four dogs keeping watch. Across the coulee and up the hillsides they spread like a noisome gray blanket. "Maa-aa, maa-aa, maa-aa," two thousand strong they blatted a strident medley while they hurried here and there after sweeter bunches of grass, very much like a disturbed ant-hill.

The herders loitered upon either slope, their dogs lying close beside them. There was good grass in that part of the coulee; the Flying U had saved it for the saddle horses that were to be gathered and held temporarily at the ranch; for it would save herding, and a week in that pasture would put a keen edge on their spirits for the hard work of the calf roundup. A dozen or two that ranged close had already been driven into the field and were feeding disdainfully in a corner as far away from the sheep as the fence would permit.

The Happy Family, riding close-grouped, stiffened in their saddles and stared amazed at the outrage.

"Sheepherders never did have any nerve," Irish observed after a minute. "They keep their places fine! They'll drive their sheep right into your dooryard and tell 'en to help themselves to anything that happens to look good to them. Oh, they're sure modest and retiring!"

Weary, who had charge of the outfit during Chip's absence, was making straight for the nearest herder. Pink and Andy went with him, as a matter of course.

"You fellows ride up around that side, and put the run on them sheep," Weary shouted back to the others. "We'll start the other side moving. Make 'em travel—back where they came from." He jerked his head toward the north. He knew, just as they all knew, that there had been no sheep to the south, unless one counted those that ranged across the Missouri river.

As the three forced their horses up the steep slope, the herder, sitting slouched upon a rock, glanced up at them dully. He had a long stick, with which he was apathetically turning over the smaller stones within his reach, and as apathetically killing the black bugs that scuttled out from the moist earth beneath. He desisted from this unexciting pastime as they drew near, and eyed them with the sullenness that comes of long isolation when the person's nature forbids that other extreme of babbling garrulity, for no man can live long months alone and remain perfectly normal. Nature, that stern mistress, always exacts a penalty from us foolish mortals who would ignore the instincts she has wisely implanted within us for our good.

"Maybe," Weary began mildly and without preface, "you don't know this is private property. Get busy with your dogs, and haze these sheep back on the bench." He waved his hand to the north. "And, when you get a good start in that direction," he added, "yuh better keep right on going."

The herder surveyed him morosely, but he said nothing; neither did he rise from the rock to obey the command. The dogs sat upon their haunches and perked their ears inquiringly, as if they understood better than did their master that these men were not to be quite overlooked.

"I meant to-day," Weary hinted, with the manner of one who deliberately holds his voice quiet.

"I never asked yuh what yuh meant," the herder mumbled, scowling. "We got to keep 'em on water another hour, yet." He went back to turning over the small rocks and to pursuing with his stick the bugs, as if the whole subject were squeezed dry of interest.

For a minute Weary stared unwinkingly down at him, uncertain whether to resent this as pure insolence, or to condone it as imbecility. "Mamma!" he breathed eloquently, and grinned at Andy and Pink. "This is a real talkative cuss, and obliging, too. Come on, boys; he's too busy to bother with a little thing like sheep."

He led the way around to the far side of the band, the nearest sheep scuttling away from then as they passed. "I don't suppose we could work the combination on those dogs—what?" he considered aloud, glancing back at them where they still sat upon their haunches and watched the strange riders. "Say, Cadwalloper, you took a few lessons in sheepherding, a couple of years ago, when you was stuck on that girl— remember? Whistle 'em up here and set 'en to work."

"You go to the devil," Pink's curved hips replied amiably to his boss. "I've got loss-uh-memory on the sheep business."

Whereat Weary grinned and said no more about it.

On the opposite side of the coulee, the boys seemed to be laboring quite as fruitlessly with the other herder. They heard Big Medicine's truculent bellow, as he leaned from the saddle and waved a fist close to the face of the herder, but, though they rode with their eyes fixed upon the group, they failed to see any resultant movement of dogs, sheep or man.

There is, at times, a certain safety in being the hopeless minority. Though seven indignant cowpunchers surrounded him, that herder was secure from any personal molestation—and he knew it. They were seven against one; therefore, after making some caustic remarks, which produced as little effect as had Weary's command upon the first man, the seven were constrained to ride here and there along the wavering, gray line, and, with shouts and swinging ropes, themselves drive the sheep from the coulee.

There was much clamor and dust and riding to and fro. There was language which would have made the mothers of then weep, and there were faces grown crimson from wrath. Eventually, however, the Happy Family faced the north fence of the Flying U boundary, and saw the last woolly back scrape under the lower wire, leaving a toll of greasy wool hanging from the barbs.

The herders had drawn together, and were looking on from a distance, and the four dogs were yelping uneasily over their enforced inaction. The Happy Family went back and rounded up the herders, and by sheer weight of numbers forced them to the fence without laying so much as a finger upon then. The one who had been killing black bugs gave then an ugly look as he crawled through, but even he did not say anything.

"Snap them wires down where they belong," Weary commanded tersely.

The man hesitated a minute, then sullenly unhooked the barbs of the two lower strands, so that the wires, which had thus been lifted to permit the passing of the sheep, twanged apart and once more stretched straight from post to post.

"Now, just keep in mind the fact that fences are built for use. This is a private ranch, and sheep are just about as welcome as smallpox. Haze them stinking things as far north as they'll travel before dark, and at daylight start 'em going again. Where's your camp, anyhow?"

"None of your business," mumbled the bugkiller sourly.

Weary scanned the undulating slope beyond the fence, saw no sign of a camp, and glanced uncertainly at his fellows. "Well, it don't matter much where it is; you see to it you don't sleep within five miles of here, or you're liable to have bad dreams. Hit the trail, now!"

They waited inside the fence until the retreating sheep lost their individuality as blatting animals, ambling erratically here and there, while they moved toward the brow of the hill, and merged into a great, gray blotch against the faint green of the new grass—a blotch from which rose again that vibrant, sing-song humming of many voices mingled. Then they rode back down the coulee to their own work, taking it for granted that the trespassing was an incident which would not be repeated—by those particular sheep, at any rate.

It was, therefore, with something of a shock that the Happy Family awoke the next morning to hear Pink's melodious treble shouting in the bunk-house at sunrise next morning:

"'G'wa-a-y round' 'em, Shep! Seven black ones in the coulee!" Men who know well the West are familiar with that facetious call.

"Ah, what's the matter with yuh?" Irish raised a rumpled, brown head from his pillow, and blinked sleepily at him. "I've been dreaming I was a sheepherder, all night."

"Well, you've got the swellest chance in the world to 'make every dream cone true, dearie,'" Pink retorted. "The whole blamed coulee's full uh sheep. I woke up a while ago and thought I just imagined I heard 'en again; so I went out to take a look—or a smell, it was—and they're sure enough there!"

Weary swung one long leg out from under his blankets and reached for his clothes. He did not say anything, but his face portended trouble for the invaders.

"Say!" cried Big Medicine, coming out of his bunk as if it were afire, "I tell yuh right now then blattin' human apes wouldn't git gay around here if I was runnin' this outfit. The way I'd have of puttin' them sheep on the run wouldn't be slow, by cripes! I'll guarantee—"

By then the bunk-house was buzzing with voices, and there was none to give heed to Big Medicine s blatant boasting. Others there were who seemed rather inclined to give Weary good advice while they pulled on their boots and sought for their gloves and rolled early-morning cigarettes, and otherwise prepared themselves for what Fate might have waiting for then outside the door.

"Are you sure they're in the coulee, Cadwalloper?" Weary asked, during a brief lull. "They could be up on the hill—"

"Hell, yes!" was Pink's forceful answer. "They could be on the hill, but they ain't. Why, darn it, they're straggling into the little pasture! I could see 'em from the stable. They—"

"Come and eat your breakfast first, boys, anyway." Weary had his hand upon the door-knob. "A few minutes more won't make any difference, one way or the other." He went out and over to the mess-house to see if Patsy had the coffee ready; for this was a good three-quarters of an hour earlier than the Flying U outfit usually bestirred themselves on these days of preparation for roundup and waiting for good grass.

"I'll be darned if I'd be as calm as he is," Cal Emmett muttered while the door was being closed. "Good thing the Old Man ain't here, now. He'd go straight up in the air. He wouldn't wait for no breakfast."

"I betche there'll be a killin' yet, before we're through with them sheep," gloomed Happy Jack. "When sheepherders starts in once to be ornery, there ain't no way uh stoppin' 'em except by killin' 'em off. And that'll mean the pen for a lot of us fellers—"

"Well, by golly, it won't be me," Slim declared loudly. "Yuh wouldn't ketch me goin' t' jail for no doggone sheepherder. They oughta be a bounty on 'en by rights."

"Seems queer they'd be right back here this morning, after being hazed out yesterday afternoon," said Andy Green thoughtfully. "Looks like they're plumb anxious to build a lot of trouble for themselves."

Patsy, thumping energetically the bottom of a tin pan, sent them trooping to the mess-house. There it was evident that the breakfast had been unduly hurried; there were no biscuits in sight, for one thing, though Patsy was lumbering about the stove frying hot-cakes. They were in too great a hurry to wait for them, however. They swallowed their coffee hurriedly, bolted a few mouthfuls of meat and fried eggs, and let it go at that.

Weary looked at then with a faint smile. "I'm going to give a few of you fellows a chance to herd sheep to-day," he announced, cooling his coffee so that it would not actually scald his palate. "That's why I wanted you to get some grub into you. Some of you fellows will have to take the trail up on the hill, and meet us outside the fence, so when we chase 'em through you can make a good job of it this time. I wonder—"

"You don't need to call out the troops for that job; one man is enough to put the fear uh the Lord into then herders," Andy remarked slightingly. "Once they're on the move—"

"All right, my boy; we'll let you be the man," Weary told him promptly. "I was going to have a bunch of you take a packadero outfit down toward Boiler Bottom and comb the breaks along there for horses—and I sure do hate to spend the whole day chasing sheepherders around over the country. So we'll haze 'em through the fence again, and, seeing you feel that way about it, I'll let you go around and keep 'em going. And, if you locate their camp, kinda impress it on the tender, if you can round him up, that the Flying U ain't pasturing sheep this spring.

No matter what kinda talk he puts up, you put the run on 'em till you see 'em across One-Man coulee. Better have Patsy put you up a lunch—unless you're fond of mutton."

Andy twisted his mouth disgustedly. "Say, I'm going to quit handing out any valuable advice to you, Weary," he expostulated.

"Haw-haw-haw-w-w!" laughed Big Medicine, and slapped Andy on the shoulder so that his face almost came in contact with his plate. "Yuh will try to work some innercent man into sheepherdin', will yuh? Haw-haw-haw-w! You'll come in tonight blattin'—if yuh don't stay out on the range tryin' t' eat grass, by cripes! Andy had a little lamb that follered him around—"

"Better let Bud take that herdin' job, Weary," Andy suggested. "It won't hurt him—he's blattin' already."

"If you think you're liable to need somebody along," Weary began, soft-heartedly relenting, "why, I guess—"

"If I can't handle two crazy sheepherders without any help, by gracious, I'll get me a job holdin' yarn in an old ladies' hone," Andy cut in hastily, and got up from the table. "Being a truthful man, I can't say I'm stuck on the job; but I'm game for it. And I'll promise you there won't be no more sheep of that brand lickin' our doorsteps. What darned outfit is it, anyway? I never bumped into any Dot sheep before, to my knowledge."

"It's a new one on me," Weary testified, heading the procession down to the stable. "If they belonged anywhere in this part of the country, though, they wouldn't be acting the way they are. They'd be wise to the fact that it ain't healthy."

Even while he spoke his eyes were fixed with cold intensity upon a fringe of gray across the coulee below the little pasture. To the nostrils of the outraged Happy Family was borne that indescribable aroma which betrays the presence of sheep; that aroma which sheepmen love and which cattlemen hate, and which a favorable wind will carry a long way.

They slapped saddles on their horses in record time that morning, and raced down the coulee ironically shouting commiserating sentences to

40

the unfortunate Andy, who rode slowly up to the mess-house for the lunch which Patsy had waiting for him in a flour sack, and afterward climbed the grade and loped along outside the line fence to a point opposite the sheep and the shouting horsemen, who forced them back by weight of numbers.

This morning the herders were not quite so passive. The bug-killer still scowled, but he spoke without the preliminary sulky silence of the day before,

"We're goin' across the coulee," he growled. "Them's orders. We range south uh here."

"No, you don't," Weary dissented calmly. "Not by a long shot, you don't. You're going back where you come from—if you ask me. And you're going quick!"

CHAPTER VI. What Happened to Andy

With the sun shining comfortably upon his back, and with a cigarette between his lips, Andy sat upon his horse and watched in silent glee while the irate Happy Family scurried here and there behind the band, swinging their ropes down upon the woolly backs, and searching their vocabularies for new and terrible epithets. Andy smiled broadly as a colorful phrase now and then boomed across the coulee in that clear, snappy atmosphere, which carries sounds so far. He did not expect to do much smiling upon his own account, that day, and he was therefore grateful for the opportunity to behold the spectacle before him.

There was Slim, for instance, unwillingly careening down hill toward home, because, in his zeal to slap an old ewe smartly with his rope, he drove her unexpectedly under his horse, and so created a momentary panic that came near standing both horse and rider upon their heads. And there was Big Medicine whistling until he was purple, while the herder, with a single gesture, held the dog motionless, though a dozen sheep

41

broke back from the band and climbed a slope so steep that Big Medicine was compelled to go after them afoot, and turn them with stones and profane objurgations.

It was very funny—when one could sit at ease upon the hilltop and smoke a cigarette while others risked apoplexy and their souls' salvation below. By the time they panted up the last rock-strewn slope of the bluff, and sent the vanguard of the invaders under the fence, Andy's mood was complacent in the extreme, and his smile offensively wide.

"Oh, you needn't look so sorry for us," drawled the Native Son, jingling over toward him until only the fence and a few feet of space divided them. "Here's where you get yours, amigo. I wish you a pleasant day—and a long one!" He waved his hand in mocking adieu, touched his horse with his silver spurs, and rode gaily away down the coulee.

"Here, sheepherder's your outfit. Ma-aa-a-a!" jeered Big Medicine. "You'll wisht, by cripes, you was a dozen men just like yuh before you're through with the deal. Haw-haw-haw-w!"

There were others who, seeing Andy's grin, had something to say upon the subject before they left.

Weary rode up, and looked undecidedly from Andy to the sheep, and back again.

"If you don't feel like tackling it single-handed, I'll send—"

"What do yuh think I am, anyway?" Andy interrupted crisply, "a Montgomery Ward two-for-a-quarter cowpuncher? Don't you fellows waste any time worrying over me!"

The herders stared at Andy curiously when he swung in behind the tail-end of the band and kept pace with their slow moving, but they did not speak beyond shouting an occasional command to their dogs. Neither did Andy have anything to say, until he saw that they were swinging steadily to the west, instead of keeping straight north, as they had been told to do. Then he rode over to the nearest herder, who happened to be the bug-killer.

"You don't want to get turned around," he hinted quietly. "That's north, over there."

"I'm workin' fer the man that pays my wages," the fellow retorted glumly, and waved an arm to a collie that was waiting for orders. The dog dropped his head, and ran around the right wing of the band, with sharp yelps and dartings here and there, turning them still more to the west.

Andy hesitated, decided to leave the man alone for the present, and rode around to the other herder.

"You swing these sheep north!" he commanded, disdaining preface or explanation.

"I'm workin' for the man that pays my wages," the herder made answer stolidly, and chewed steadily upon a quid of tobacco that had stained his lips unbecomingly.

So they had talked the thing over—had those two herders—and were following a premeditated plan of defiance! Andy hooked at the man a minute. "You turn them sheep, damn you," he commanded again, and laid a hand upon his saddle-horn suggestively.

"You go to the devil, damn yuh," advised the herder, and cocked a wary eye at him from under his hat-brim. Not all herders, let it be said in passing, take unto themselves the mental attributes of their sheep; there are those who believe that a bold front is better than weak compliance, and who will back that belief by a very bold front indeed.

Andy appraised him mentally, decided that he was an able-bodied man and therefore fightable, and threw his right leg over the cantle with a quite surprising alacrity.

"Are you going to turn them sheep?" Andy was taking off his coat when he made that inquiry.

"Not for your tellin'. You keep back, young feller, or I'll sick the dogs on yuh." He turned and whistled to the nearest one, and Andy hit him on the ear.

They clinched and pummeled when they could and where they could. The dog came up, circled the gyrating forms twice, then sat down upon his haunches at a safe distance, tilted his head sidewise and lifted his ears interestedly. He was a wise little dog; the other dog was also wise, and remained phlegmatically at his post, as did the bug-killer.

"Are you going to turn them sheep?" Andy spoke breathlessly, but with deadly significance.

"N-yes."

Andy took his fingers from the other's Adam's apple, his knee from the other's diaphragm, and went over to where he had thrown down his coat, felt in a pocket for his handkerchief, and, when he had found it, applied it to his nose, which was bleeding profusely.

"Fly at it, then," he advised, eyeing the other sternly over the handkerchief. "I'd hate to ask you a third time."

"I'd hate to have yuh," conceded the herder reluctantly. "I was sure I c'd lick yuh, or I'd 'a' turned 'em before." He sent the dog racing down the south line of the band.

Andy got thoughtfully back upon his horse, and sat looking hard at the herder. "Say, you're grade above the general run uh lamb-hickers," he observed, after a minute. "Who are you working for, and what's your object in throwing sheep on Flying U land? There's plenty of range to the north."

"I'm workin'," said the herder, "for the Dot outfit. I thought you could read brands."

"Don't get sassy—I've got a punch or two I haven't used yet. Who owns these woollies?"

"Well—Whittaker and Oleson, if yuh want to know."

"I do." Andy was keeping pace with him around the band, which edged off from then and the dogs. "And what makes you so crazy about Flying U grass?" he pursued.

"We've got to cross that coulee to git to where we're headed for; we got a right to, and we're going to do it." The herder paused and glanced up at Andy sourly. "We knowed you was a mean outfit; the boss told us so. And he told us you was blank ca'tridges and we needn't back up just 'cause you raised up on your hind legs and howled a little. I've had truck with you cowmen before. I've herded sheep in Wyoming." He walked a few steps with his head down, considering.

"I better go over and talk some sense into the other fellow," he said, looking up at Andy as if all his antagonism had oozed in the fight. "You ride along this edge, so they won't scatter—we ought to be grazin' 'em along, by rights; only you seem to be in such an all-fired rush—"

"You go on and tell that loco son-of-a-gun over there what he's up against," Andy urged. "Blank cartridges—I sure do like that! If you only knew it, high power dum-dums would be a lot closer to our brand. Run along—I am in a kinda hurry, this morning."

Andy, riding slowly upon the outskirts of the grazing, blatting band, watched the two confer earnestly together a hundred yards or so away. They seemed to be having some sort of argument; the bug-killer gesticulated with the long stick he carried, and the sheep, while the herders talked, scattered irresponsibly. Andy wondered what made sheepmen so "ornery," particularly herders. He wondered why the fellow he had thrashed was so insultingly defiant at first, and, after the thrashing, so unresentful and communicative, and so amenable to authority withal. He felt his nose, and decided that it was, all things considered, a cheap victory, and yet one of which he need not be ashamed.

The herder cane back presently and helped drive the sheep over the edge of the bluff which bordered Antelope coulee. The bug-killer, upon his side, also seemed imbued with the spirit of obedience; Andy heard him curse a collie into frenzied zeal, and smiled approvingly.

"Now you're acting a heap more human," he observed; and the man from Wyoming grinned ruefully by way of reply.

Antelope coulee, at that point, was steep; too steep for riding, so that Andy dismounted and dug his boot-heels into the soft soil, to gain a foothold on the descent. When he was halfway down, he chanced to look back, straight into the scowling gaze of the bug-killer, who was sliding down behind him.

"Thought you were hazing down the other side of 'em," Andy called back, but the herder did not choose to answer save with another scowl.

Andy edged his horse around an impracticable slope of shale stuff and went on. The herder followed. When he was within twelve feet or so of the bottom, there was a sound of pebbles knocked loose in haste, a scrambling, and then came the impact of his body. Andy teetered, lost his balance, and went to the bottom in one glorious slide. He landed with the bug-killer on top—and the bug-killer failed to remove his person as speedily as true courtesy exacted.

Andy kicked and wriggled and tried to remember what was that high-colored, vituperative sentence that Irish had invented over a stubborn sheep, that he might repeat it to the bug-killer. The herder from Wyoming ran up, caught Andy's horse, and untied Andy's rope from the saddle.

"Good fer you, Oscar," he praised the bug-killer. "Hang onto him while I take a few turns." He thereupon helped force Andy's arms to his side, and wound the rope several times rather tightly around Andy's outraged, squirming person.

"Oh, it ain't goin' to do yuh no good to buck 'n bawl," admonished the tier. "I learnt this here little trick down in Wyoming. A bunch uh punchers done it to me—and I've been just achin' all over fer a chance to return the favor to some uh you gay boys. And," he added, with malicious satisfaction, while he rolled Andy over and tied a perfectly unslippable knot behind, "it gives me great pleasure to hand the dose out to you, in p'ticular. If I was a mean man, I'd hand yuh the boot a few times fer luck; but I'll save that up till next time."

"You can bet your sweet life there'll be a next time," Andy promised earnestly, with embellishments better suited to the occasion than to a children's party.

"Well, when it arrives I'm sure Johnny-on-the-spot. Them Wyoming punchers beat me up after they'd got me tied. I'm tellin' yuh so you'll see I ain't mean unless I'm drove to it. Turn him feet down hill, Oscar, so he won't git a rush uh brains to the head and die on our hands. Now you're goin' to mind your own business, sonny. Next time yuh set out to herd sheep, better see the boss first and git on the job right."

He rose to his feet, surveyed Andy with his hands on his hips, mentally pronounced the job well done, and took a generous chew of tobacco, after which he grinned down at the trussed one.

"That the language uh flowers you're talkin'?" he inquired banteringly, before he turned his attention to the horse, which he disposed of by tying up the reins and giving it a slap on the rump. When it had trotted fifty yards down the coulee bottom, and showed a disposition to go farther, he whistled to his dogs, and turned again to Andy.

"This here is just a hint to that bunch you trot with, to leave us and our sheep alone," he said. "We don't pick no quarrels, but we're goin' to cross our sheep wherever we dern please, to git where we want to go. Gawd didn't make this range and hand it over to you cowmen to put in yer pockets—I guess there's a chance fer other folks to hang on by their eyebrows, anyway."

Andy, lying there like a very good presentation of a giant cocoon, roped round and round, with his arms pinned to his sides, had the doubtful pleasure of seeing that noisome, foolish-faced band trail down Antelope coulee and back upon the level they had just left, and of knowing to a gloomy certainty that he could do nothing about it, except swear; and even that palls when a man has gone over his entire repertoire three times in rapid succession.

Andy, therefore, when the last sheep had trotted out of sight, hearing and smell, wriggled himself into as comfortable a position as his bonds would permit, and took a nap.

CHAPTER VII. Truth Crushed to Earth, etc.

Andy, only half awake, tried to obey both instinct and habit and reach up to pull his hat down over his eyes, so that the sun could not shine upon his lids so hotly; when he discovered that he could do no more than wiggle his fingers, he came back with a jolt to reality and tried to sit up.

It is surprising to a man to discover suddenly just how important a part his arms play in the most simple of body movements; Andy, with his arms pinioned tightly the whole length of them, rolled over on his face, kicked a good deal, and rolled back again, but he did not sit up, as he had confidently expected to do.

He lay absolutely quiet for at least five minutes, staring up at the brilliant blue arch above him. Then he began to speak rapidly and earnestly; a man just close enough to hear his voice sweeping up to a certain rhetorical climax, pausing there and commencing again with a rhythmic fluency of intonation, might have thought that he was repeating poetry; indeed, it sounded like some of Milton's majestic blank verse, but it was not. Andy was engaged in a methodical, scientific, reprehensibly soul-satisfying period of swearing.

A curlew, soaring low, with long beak outstretched before him, and long legs outstretched behind cast a beady eye upon him, and shrilled "Cor-reck! Cor-reck!" in unregenerate approbation of the blasphemy.

Andy stopped suddenly and laughed. "Glad you agree with me, old sport," he addressed the bird whimsically, with a reaction to his normally cheerful outlook. "Sheepherders are all those things I named over, birdie, and some that I can't think of at present."

He tried again, this time with a more careful realization of his limitations, to assume an upright position; and being a persevering young man, and one with a ready wit, he managed at length to wriggle himself back upon the slope from which he had slid in his sleep, and, by digging in his heels and going carefully, he did at last rise upon his knees, and from there triumphantly to his feet.

He had at first believed that one of the herders would, in the course of an hour or so, return and untie him, when he hoped to be able to retrieve, in a measure, his self-respect, which he had lost when the first three feet of his own rope had encircled him. To be tied and trussed by sheepherders! Andy gritted his teeth and started down the coulee.

He was hungry, and his lunch was tied to his saddle. He looked eagerly down the coulee, in the faint hope of seeing his horse grazing somewhere along its length, until the numbness of his arms and hands reminded him that forty lunches, tied upon forty saddles at his side, would be of no use to him in his present position. His hands he could not move from his thighs; he could wiggle his fingers—which he did, to relieve as much as possible that unpleasant, prickly sensation which we call a "going to sleep" of the afflicted members. When it occurred to him that he could not do anything with his horse if he found it, he gave up looking for it and started for the ranch, walking awkwardly, because of his bonds, the sun shining hotly upon his brown head, because his hat had been knocked off in the scuffle, and he could not pick it up and put it back where it belonged.

Taking a straight course across the prairie, he struck Flying U coulee at the point where the sheep had left it. On the way there he had crossed their trail where they went through the fence farther along the coulee than before, and therefore with a better chance of passing undetected; especially since the Happy Family, believing that he was forcing them steadily to the north, would not be watching for sheep. The barbed wire barrier bothered him somewhat. He was compelled to lie down and roll under the fence, in the most undignified manner, and, when he was through, there was the problem of getting upon his feet again. But he managed it somehow, and went on down the coulee, perspiring with the heat and a bitter realization of his ignominy. What the Happy Family would have to say when they saw him, even Andy Green's vivid imagination declined to picture.

He knew by the sun that it was full noon when he came in sight of the stable and corrals, and his soul sickened at the thought of facing that derisive bunch of punchers, with their fiendish grins and their barbed tongues. But he was hungry, and his arms had reached the limit of prickly sensations and were numb to his shoulders. He shook his hair back from his beaded forehead, cast a wary glance at the silent stables, set his jaw, and went on up the hill to the mess-house, wishing tardily that he had waited until they were off at work again, when he might intimidate old Patsy into keeping quiet about his predicament.

Within the mess-house was the clatter of knives and forks plied by hungry men, the sound of desultory talk and a savory odor of good things to eat. The door was closed. Andy stood before it as a guilty-conscienced child stands before its teacher; clicked his teeth together, and, since he could not open the door, lifted his right foot and gave it a kick to strain the hinges.

Within were exclamations of astonishment, silence and then a heavy tread. Patsy opened the door, gasped and stood still, his eyes popping out like a startled rabbit.

"Well, what's eating you?" Andy demanded querulously, and pushed past him into the room.

Not all of the Happy Family were there. Cal, Jack Bates, Irish and Happy Jack had gone into the Bad Lands next to the river; but there were enough left to make the soul of Andy quiver forebodingly, and to send the flush of extreme humiliation to his cheeks.

The Happy Family looked at him in stunned surprise; then they glanced at one another in swift, wordless inquiry, grinned wisely and warily, and went on with their dinner. At least they pretended to go on with their dinner, while Andy glared at them with amazed reproach in his misleadingly honest gray eyes.

"When you've got plenty of time," he said at last in a choked tone, "maybe one of you obliging cusses will untie this damned rope."

"Why, sure!" Pink threw a leg over the bench and got up with cheerful alacrity. "I'll do it now, if you say so; I didn't know but what that was some new fad of yours, like—"

"Fad!" Andy repeated the word like an explosion.

"Well, by golly, Andy needn't think I'm goin' to foller that there style," Slim stated solemnly. "I need m' rope for something else than to tie n' clothes on with."

"I sure do hate to see a man wear funny things just to make himself conspicuous," Pink observed, while he fumbled at the knot, which was intricate. Andy jerked away from him that he might face him ragefully.

"Maybe this looks funny to you," he cried, husky with wrath. "But I can't seem to see the joke, myself. I admit I let then herders make a monkey of me.... They slipped up behind, going down into Antelope coulee, and slid down the bluff onto me; and, before I could get up, they got me tied, all right. I licked one of 'en before that, and thought I had 'en gentled down—"

Andy stopped short, silenced by that unexplainable sense which warns us when our words are received with cold disbelief.

"Mh-hm—I thought maybe you'd run up against a hostile jackrabbit, or something," Pink purred, and went back to his place on the bench.

"Haw-haw-haw-w-w!" came Big Medicine's tardy bellow. "That's more reasonable than the sheepherder story, by cripes!"

Andy looked at them much as he had stared up at the sky before he began to swear—speechlessly, with a trembling of the muscles around his mouth. He was quite white, considering how tanned he was, and his forehead was shiny, with beads of perspiration standing thickly upon it.

"Weary, I wish you'd untie this rope. I can't." He spoke still in that peculiar, husky tone, and, when the last words were out, his teeth went together with a snap.

Weary glanced inquiringly across at the Native Son, who was regarding Andy steadily, as one gazes upon a tangled rope, looking for the end which will easiest lead to an untangling.

Miguel's brown eyes turned languidly to meet the look. "You'd better untie him," he advised in his soft drawl. "He may not be in the habit of doing it—but he's telling the truth."

"Untie me, Miguel," begged Andy, going over to him, "and let me at this bunch."

"I'll do it," said Weary, and rose pacifically. "I kinda believe you myself, Andy. But you can't blame the boys none; you've fooled 'em till they're dead shy of anything they can't see through. And, besides, it sure does look like a plant. I'd back you single-handed against a dozen sheepherders like then two we've been chasing around. If I hadn't felt that way I wouldn't have sent yuh out alone with 'em."

"Well, Andy needn't think he's goin' to stick me on that there story," Slim declared with brutal emphasis. "I've swallered too many baits, by golly. He's figurin' on gettin' us all out on the war-path, runnin' around in circles, so's't he can give us the laugh. I'll bet, by golly, he paid then herders to tie him up like that. He can't fool me!"

"Say, Slim, I do believe your brains is commencin' to sprout!" Big Medicine thumped him painfully upon the back by way of accenting the compliment. "You got the idee, all right."

Andy stood quiet while Weary unwound the rope; lifted his numbed arms with some difficulty, and displayed to the doubters his rope-creased wrists, and purple, swollen hands.

"I couldn't fight a caterpiller right now," he said thickly. "Look at them hands! Do yuh call that a josh? I've been tied up like a bed-roll for five hours, you—" Well, never mind, he merely repeated a part of what he had recited aloud in Antelope coulee, the only difference being that he applied the vitriolic utterances to the Happy Family instead of to sheepherders, and that with the second recitation he gained much in fluency and dramatic delivery.

It is not nice for a man to swear; to swear the way Andy did, at any rate. But the result perhaps atoned in a measure for the wickedness, in that the Happy Family were absolutely convinced of his sincerity, and the feelings of Andy greatly relieved, so that, when he had for the third time that day completely exhausted his vocabulary, he sat down and began to eat his dinner with a keen appetite.

"I don't suppose you know where your horse is at, by this tine," Weary observed, as casually as possible, breaking a somewhat constrained silence.

"I don't—and I don't give a darn," Andy snapped back. He ate a few mouthfuls, and added less savagely: "He wasn't in sight, as I came along. I didn't follow the trail; I struck straight across and came down the coulee. He may be at the gate, and he may be down toward Rogers'."

Pink reached for a toothpick, eyeing Andy side-long; dimpled his cheeks disarmingly, and cleared his throat. "Please don't kill me off when you get that pie swallowed," he began pacifically. "Strange as it may seem, I believe you, Andy. What I want to know is this: Who owns them Dots? And what are they chasing all over the Flying U range for? It looks plumb malicious, to me. Did you find out anything about 'en,

Andy, while you—er—while they—" His eyes twinkled and betrayed him for an arrant pretender. (Pink was not afraid of anything on earth—least of all Andy Green.)

"I will kill yuh by inches, if I hear any remarks out of yuh that ain't respectful," Andy promised, thawing to his normal tone, which was pleasant to the ear. "I didn't find out much about 'em. The fellow I licked told me that Whittaker and Oleson owned the sheep. He didn't say—"

"Well—by—golly!" Shin thrust his head forward belligerently. "Whittaker! Well, what d'yuh think uh that!" He glared from one face to the other, his gaze at last resting upon Weary. "Say, do yuh reckon it's—Dunk?"

Weary paid no heed to Slim. He leaned forward, his face turned to Andy with that concentration of attention which means so much more than mere exclamation. "You're sure he said Whittaker?" he asked.

His tone and his attitude arrested Andy's cup midway to his mouth. "Sure—Whittaker and Oleson. I never heard of the outfit—who's this Whittaker person?"

Weary settled back in his place and smiled, but his eyes had quite lost their habitually sunny expression.

"Up until four years ago," he explained evenly, "he was the Old Man's partner. We caught him in some mighty dirty work, and—well, he sold out to the Old Man. The old party with the hoofs and tail can't be everywhere at once, the way I've got it sized up, so he turns some of his business over to other folks. Dunk Whittaker's his top hand."

"Why, by golly, he framed up a job on the Gordon boys, and railroaded 'em to the pen, just—"

"Oh, that's the gazabo!" Andy's eyes shone with enlightenment. "I've heard a lot about Dunk, but I didn't know his last name—"

"Say! I'll bet they're the outfit that bought out Denson. That's why old Denson acted so queer, maybe. Selling to a sheep outfit would make the old devil feel kinda uneasy, talking to us—" Pink's eyes were big and purple with excitement. "And that train-load of sheep we saw Sunday, I'll bet is the same identical outfit."

"Dunk Whittaker'd better not try to monkey with me, by golly!" Slim's face was lowering. "And he'd better not monkey with the Flying U either. I'd pump him so full uh holes he'd look like a colander, by golly!"

Weary got up and started to the door, his face suddenly grown careworn. "Slim, you and Miguel better go and hunt up Andy's horse," he said with a hint of abstraction in his tone, as though his mind was busy with more important things. "Maybe Andy'll feel able to help you set those posts, Bud—and you'd better go along the upper end of the little pasture with the wire stretchers and tighten her up; the top wire is pretty loose, I noticed this morning." His fingers fumbled with the door-knob.

"Want me to do anything?" Pink asked quizzically just behind him. "I thought sure we'd go and remonstrate with then gay—"

Weary interrupted him. "The herders can wait—and, anyway, I've kinda got an idea Andy wants to hand out his own brand of poison to that bunch. You and I will take a ride over to Denson's and see what's going on over there. Mamma!" he added fervently, under his breath, "I sure do wish Chip and the Old Man were here!"

CHAPTER VIII. The Dot Outfit

Before he laid him down to sleep, that night, Weary had repeated to himself many times and fervently that wish for old J. G. Whitmore and the stout staff upon which he was beginning more and more to lean, his brother-in-law, Chip Bennett. As matters stood, Weary could not even bring himself to let then know anything about his trouble—and that the thing was beginning to assume the form and shape and general malevolent attributes of Trouble, Weary was forced to admit to himself.

Just at present an unthinking, unobserving person might pass over this sheep outfit as a mere unsavory incident; but Weary was neither unobserving nor unthinking—nor, for the matter of that, were the rest of the Happy Family. It needed no Happy Jack, with his foreboding nature, to point out the unpleasant possibilities that night when the committee of two made their informal report at the supper table.

They had ridden to Denson coulee, which was in reality a meandering branch of Flying U coulee itself. To reach it one rode out of Flying U coulee and over a wide hill, and down again to Denson's. But the creek—Flying U creek—followed the devious turnings from Denson coulee down to the Flying U. A long mile of Flying U coulee J. G. Whitmore owned outright. Another mile he held under no other title save a fence. The creek flowed through it all—but that creek had its source somewhere up near the head of Denson coulee. J. G. Whitmore had, to his regret, been unable to claim the whole earth—or at least that portion of it—for his own; so, when he was constrained to make a choice, he settled himself in the wider, more fertile coulee, which he thereafter called the Flying U. While it is good policy to locate as near as possible to the source of those erratic little creeks which water certain garden spots of the northern range land, it is also well to choose land that will grow plenty of hay. J. G. Whitmore chose the hay land, and trusted that providence would insure the water supply. Through all these years Flying U creek had never once disappointed him. Denson, who settled in the tributary coulee, had not made any difference in the water supply, and his stock had consisted of thirty or forty head of cattle and horses.

When Denson sold, however, things might be different. And, if he had sold to a sheepman, the change might be unpleasant If he had sold to Dunk Whittaker—the Flying U boys faced that possibility just as they would face any other disaster, undaunted, but grim and unsmiling.

It was thus that Pink and Weary rode slowly down into Denson coulee. Two miles back they had passed the band of Dot sheep, feeding leisurely just without the Flying U fence, which was the southern boundary. The bug-killer and the other were there, and they noted that the features of that other bore witness to the truth of Andy's story of the fight. He regarded them with one perfectly good eye and one which was considerably swollen, and grinned a swollen grin.

The two had ridden ten paces past him when Pink pulled up suddenly. "I'm going to get off and lick that son-of-a-gun myself, just for luck," he stated dispassionately. "I'm going to lick 'em both," he revised while he dismounted.

"Oh, come on, Cadwalloper," Weary dissuaded. "You'll likely have all the excitement you need, without that."

"Here, you hold this fool cayuse. No." He shook his head, cutting short further protest. "You're the boss, and you don't want to mix in, and that part is all right. But I ain't responsible—and I sure am going to take a fall or two out of these geesers. They're a-w-l together too stuck on themselves to suit me." Pink did not say that he was thinking of Andy, but nevertheless a vivid recollection of that unfortunate young man's rope-creased wrists and swollen hands sent him toward the herder with long, eager strides.

Pink was not tall, and he was slight and boyish of build; also, his cherubic face, topped by tawny curls and lighted by eyes as deeply blue and as innocent as a baby's, probably deceived that herder, just as they had deceived many another. For Pink was a good deal like a stick of dynamite wrapped in white tissue paper and tied with blue ribbon; and Weary was not at all uneasy over the outcome, as he watched Pink go clanking back, though he loved him well.

Pink did not waste any time or words on the preliminaries. With a delightful frankness of purpose he pulled off his coat and threw it on the ground, as he came up, sent his hat after it, and arrived fist first.

The herder had waited grinning, and he had shouted something to Weary about spanking the kid if Weary didn't make him behave. Speedily he became a very surprised herder, and a distressed one as well.

"All right," Pink remarked, a little quick-breathed, when the herder decided for the third time to get up. "A friend of mine worked yuh over a little, this morning, and I just thought I'd make a better job than he did. Your eyes didn't match. They will, now."

The herder mumbled maledictions after him, but Pink would not even give him the satisfaction of resenting it.

"I'd like to have broken a knuckle against his teeth, darn him," he observed ruefully when he was in the saddle again. "Come on, Weary. It won't take but a minute to hand a punch or two to that bug-killer, and then I'll feel better. They've both got it coming—come on!" This because Weary showed a strong inclination to take the trail and keep it to his destination. "Well, I'll go alone, then. I've got to kinda square myself for the way I threw it into Andy; and you know blamed well, Weary, they played it low-down on him, or they'd never have got that rope on him. And I'm going to lick that—"

"Mamma! You sure are a rambunctious person when you feel that way," Weary made querulous comment; but he rode over with Pink to where the bug-killer was standing with his long stick held in a somewhat menacing manner, and once more he held Pink's horse for him.

Pink was gone longer this time, and he came back with a cut lip and a large lump on his forehead; the bug-killer had thrown a small rock with the precision which comes of much practice—such as stoning disobedient dogs, and the like—and, when Pink rushed at him furiously, the herder caught him very neatly alongside the head with his stick. These little amenities serving merely to whet Pink's appetite for battle, he stopped long enough to thrash that particular herder very thoroughly and to his own complete satisfaction.

"Well, I guess I'm ready to go on now," he observed, dimpling rather one-sidedly as he got back on his horse.

"I thought maybe you'd want to whip the dogs, too," Weary told him dryly; which was the nearest he came to expressing any disapproval of the incident. Weary was a peace-loving soul, whenever peace was compatible with self-respect; and it would never have occurred to him to punish strange men as summarily as Pink had done.

"I would, if the dogs were half as ornery as the men," Pink retorted. "Say, they hang together like bull snakes and rattlers, don't they? If they was human, they'd have helped each other out—but nothing doing! Do you reckon a man could ride up to a couple of our bunch, and thrash one at a time without the other fellow having something to say about it?" He turned in the saddle and looked back. "So help me, Josephine, I've got a good mind to go back and lick them again, for not hanging together like they ought to." But the threat was an idle one, and they went on to Denson's, Weary still with that anxious look in his eyes, and Pink quite complacent over his exploit.

In Denson coulee was an unwonted atmosphere of activity; heretofore the place had been animated chiefly by young Densons engaged in the pursuit of pleasure, but now a covered buggy, evidently just arrived, bore mute witness to the new order of things. There were more horses about the place, a covered wagon or two, three or four men working upon the corral, and, lastly, there was one whom Weary recognized the moment he caught sight of him.

"Looks like a sheep outfit, all right," he said somberly. "And, if that ain't old Dunk himself, it's the devil, and that's next thing to him."

Dunk, they judged, had just arrived with another man whom they did not know: a tall man with light hair that hung lank to his collar, a thin, sharp-nosed face and a wide mouth, which stretched easily into a smile, but which was none the pleasanter for that. When he turned inquiringly toward them they saw that he was stoop-shouldered; though not from any deformity, but from sheer, slouching lankness. Dunk gave them a swift, sour look from under his eyebrows and went on.

Weary rode straight past the lank man, whom he judged to be Oleson, and overtook Dunk Whittaker himself.

"Hello, Dunk," he said cheerfully, sliding over in the saddle so that a foot hung free of the stirrup, as men who ride much have learned to do when they stop for a chat, thereby resting while they may. "Back on the old stamping ground, are you?"

"Since you see me here, I suppose I am," Dunk made churlish response.

"Do you happen to own those Dot sheep, back there on the hill?" Weary tilted his head toward home.

"I happen to own half of them." By then they had reached the gate and Dunk passed through and started on to the house.

"Oh, don't be in a rush—come on back and be sociable," Weary called out, in the mildest of tones, twisting the reins around his saddle-horn so that he might roll a cigarette at ease.

Dunk remembered, perhaps, certain things he had learned when he was J. G. Whitmore's partner, and had more or less to do with the charter members of the Happy Family. He came back and stood by the gate, ungraciously enough, to be sure; still, he came back. Weary smiled under cover of lighting his cigarette. Dunk, by that reluctant compliance, betrayed something which Weary had been rather anxious to know.

"We've been having a little trouble with those sheep of yours," Weary remarked between puffs. "You've got some poor excuses for humans herding them. They drove the bunch across our coulee just exactly three times. There ain't enough grass left in our lower field to graze a prairie dog." He glanced back to see where Pink was, saw that he was close behind, as was the lank man, and spoke in a tone that included them all.

"The Flying U ain't pasturing sheep, this spring," he informed them pleasantly. "But, seeing the grass is eat up, we'll let yuh pay for it. Why didn't you bring them in along the trail, anyway?"

"I didn't bring them in. I just came down from Butte to-day. I suppose the herders brought them out where the feed was best; they did if they're worth their wages."

"They happened to strike some feed that was pretty expensive. And," he smiled down at Whittaker misleadingly, "you ought to keep an eye on those herders, or they might let you in for another grass bill. The Flying U has got quite a lot of range, right around here, you recollect. And we've got plenty of cattle to eat it. We don't need any help to keep the grass down so we can ride through it."

"Now, look here," began the lank man with that sort of persuasiveness which can turn instantly into bluster, "all this is pure foolishness, you know. We're here to stay. We've bought this place, and some other land to go with it, and we expect to stay right here and make a living. It happens that we expect to make a living off of sheep. Now, we don't want to start in by quarreling with our neighbors, and we don't want our neighbors to start any quarrel with us. All we want—"

"Mamma! You're taking a fine way to make us love yuh," Weary cut in ironically. "I know what you want. You want the same as every other meek and lovely sheepman wants. You want it all—core, seeds and peeling. Dunk," he said with a more impatient disgust than he was in the habit of showing for his fellowmen, "this man's a stranger; but I should think you'd know better than to come in here with sheep."

"I don't know why a sheep outfit isn't exactly as good as a cow outfit, and I don't know why they haven't as much right here. You're welcome to what land you own, but it always seemed to me that public land is open to the use of the public. Now, as Oleson says, we expect to raise sheep here, and we expect your outfit to leave us alone. As far as our sheep crossing your coulee is concerned—I don't know that they did. But, if they did, and, if they did any damage, let J. G. do the talking about that. I deal with the owners—not with the hired men."

Weary, you must understand, was never a bellicose young man. But, for all that, he leaned over and gave Dunk a slap on the jaw which must have stung considerably—and the full reason for his violence lay four years behind the two, when Dunk was part owner of the Flying U, and when his sneering arrogance had been very hard to endure.

"Are you going to swallow that—from a hired man?" Weary inquired, after a minute during which nothing whatever occurred beyond the slow reddening of Dunk's face.

"I'm not going to fight, if that's what you mean," Dunk sneered. "I decline to bring myself down to your level. One doesn't expect anything from a jackass but a bray, you know—and one doesn't feel compelled to bray because the jackass does." He smiled that supercilious smile which Weary had hated of old, and which, he knew, was well used to covering much treachery and small meannesses of various sorts.

"As I said, if the Flying U has any claim against us, let the owner present it in the usual way." Dunk drew down his black brows, lifted a corner of his lip and turned his back deliberately upon them.

Oleson let himself through the gate, which he closed somewhat hastily behind him. "I'm sorry you fellows seem to want to make trouble," he said, without looking up from the latch, which seemed somewhat out of repair, like the rest of the Denson property. "That's a poor way to start in with new neighbors." He lifted his hat with what Pink considered insulting politeness, and followed Dunk into the house.

Weary waited there until they had gone in and closed the door, then turned and rode back home again, frowning thoughtfully at the trail ahead of them all the way, and making no reply to Pink's importunings for war.

"I'd hate to say you've lost your nerve, Weary," Pink cried at last, in sheer desperation. "But why the devil didn't you get down and thump the daylights out of that black son-of-a-gun? I came pretty near walking into him myself, only I hate to butt into another fellow's scrap. But, if I'd known you were going to set there and let him walk off with that sneer on his face—"

"I can't fight a man that won't hit back," Weary protested. "You couldn't either, Cadwalloper. You'd have done just what I did; you'd have let him go."

"He will hit back, all right enough," Pink retorted passionately. "He'll do it when you ain't looking, though. He—"

"I know it," Weary sighed. "I'm kinda sorry, now, I slapped him. He'll hit back—but he won't hit me; he'll aim at the outfit. If the Old Man was here, or Chip, I'd feel a whole lot easier in my mind."

"They couldn't do anything you can't do," Pink assured him loyally, forgetting his petulance when he saw the careworn look in Weary's face. "All they can do is gobble all the range around here—and I guess there's a few of us that will have a word or two to say about that."

"What makes me sore," Weary confided, "is knowing that Dunk isn't thinking altogether of the dollar end of it. He's tickled to death to get a whack at the outfit. And I hate to see him get away with it; but I guess we'll have to stand for it."

That sentiment did not please Pink; nor, when Weary repeated it later that evening in the bunk-house, did it please the Happy Family. The less pleasing it was because it was perfectly true and every man of them knew it. Beyond keeping the sheep off Flying U land, there was nothing they could do without stepping over the line into lawlessness—and, while they were not in any sense a meek Happy Family, they were far more law-abiding than their conversation that night made them appear.

CHAPTER IX. More Sheep

The next week was a time of harassment for the Flying U; a week filled to overflowing with petty irritations, traceable, directly or indirectly, to their new neighbors, the Dot sheepmen. The band in charge of the bug-chaser and that other unlovable man from Wyoming fed just as close to the Flying U boundary as their guardians dared let them feed; a great deal closer than was good for the tempers of the Happy Family, who rode fretfully here and there upon their own business and at the same time tried to keep an eye upon their unsavory neighbors—a proceeding as nerve-racking as it was futile.

The Native Son, riding home in jingling haste from Dry Lake, whither he had hurried one afternoon in the hope of cheering news from Chicago, reported another trainload of Dots on the wide level beyond Antelope coulee. There were, he said, four men in charge of the band, and he believed they carried guns, though he was not positive of that. They were moving slowly, and he thought they would not attempt to cross Flying U coulee before the next day; though, from the course they were taking, he was sure they meant to cross.

Coupled with that bit of ill-tidings, the brief note from Chip, saying very little about the Old Man, but implying a good deal by its very omissions, would have been enough to send the Happy Family to sleepless beds that night if they had been the kind to endure with silent fortitude their troubles.

"If you fellers would back me up," brooded Big Medicine down by the corral after supper, "I'd see to it them sheep never gits across the coulee, by cripes! I'd send 'em so far the other way they'd git plumb turned around and forgit they ever wanted to go south."

"It's all Dunk's devilishness," Jack Bates declared. "He could take them in the other way, even if the feed ain't so good along the trail. It's most all prairie-dog towns—but that's good enough for sheep." Jack, in his intense partisanship, spoke as if sheep were not entitled to decent grass at any time or under any circumstances.

"Them herders packin' guns looks to me like they're goin' to make trouble if they kin," gloomed Happy Jack. "I betche they'll kill somebody before they're through. When sheepmen gits mean—"

Pink picked up his rope and started for the large corral, where a few saddle horses had been driven in just before supper and had not yet been turned out.

"You fellows can stand around and chew the rag, if you want to," he said caustically, "and wait for Weary to make a war-talk. But I'm going to keep cases on them Dots, if I have to stand an all-night guard on 'em. I don't blame Weary; he's looking out for the law-and-order business—and that's all right. But I'm not in charge of the outfit. I'm going to do as I darn please, and, if they don't like my style, they can give me my time."

"Good for you, Little One!" Big Medicine hurried to overtake him so that he might slap him on the shoulder with his favorite, sledge-hammer method of signifying his approval of a man's sentiments. "Honest to grandma, I was just b'ginnin' to think this bunch was gitting all streaked up with yeller. 'Course, we ain't goin' to wait for no official orders, by cripes! I'd ruther lock Weary up in the blacksmith shop than let him tell us to go ahead. Go awn and tell him a good, stiff lie, Andy—just to keep him interested while us fellers make a gitaway. He ain't in on this; we don't want him in on it."

"What yuh goin' to do?" Happy Jack inquired suspiciously. "Yuh can't go and monkey with them sheep, er them herders. They ain't on our land. And, if you don't git killed, old Dunk'll fix yuh like he fixed the Gordon boys—I know him—to a fare-you-well. It'd tickle him to death to git something on us fellers. I betche that's what he's aiming t'do. Git us to fightin' his outfit so's't—"

"Oh, go off and lie down!" Andy implored him contemptuously. "We're going to hang those herders, and drive the sheep all over a cutback somewhere, like Jesus done to the hogs, and then we're going over and murder old Dunk, if he's at home, and burn the house to hide the guilty deed. And, if the sheriff comes snooping around, asking disagreeable questions, we'll all swear you done it. So now you know our plans; shut your face and go on to bed. And be sure," he added witheringly, "you pull the soogans over your head, so you won't hear the dying shriek of our victims. We're liable to get kinda excited and torture 'em a while before we kill 'em."

"Aw, gwan!" gulped Happy Jack mechanically. "You make me sick! If yuh think I'm goin' to swaller all that, you're away off! You wouldn't dast do nothing of the kind; and, if yuh did, you'd sure have a sweet time layin' it onto me!"

"Oh, I don't know," drawled the Native Son, with a slow, velvet-eyed glance, "any jury in the country would hang you on your looks, Happy. I knew a man down in the lower part of California, who was arrested, tried and hanged for murder. And all the evidence there was against him was the fact that he was seen within five miles of the place on the same day the murder was committed; and his face. They had an expert physiognomist there, and he swore that the fellow had the face of a murderer; the poor devil looked like a criminal—and, though he had one of the best lawyers on the Coast, it was adios for him."

"I s'pose you mean I got the face of a criminal!" sputtered Happy Jack. "It ain't always the purty fellers that wins out—like you 'n' Pink. I never seen the purty man yit that was worth the powder it'd take to blow him up! Aw, you fellers make me sick!" He went off, muttering his opinion of them all, and particularly of the Native Son, who smiled while he listened. "You go awn and start something—and you'll wisht you hadn't," they heard him croak from the big gate, and chuckled over his wrath.

As a matter of fact, the Happy Family, as a whole, or as individuals, had no intention of committing any great violence that evening. Pink wanted to see just where this new band of sheep was spending the night, and to find out, if possible, what were the herders' intentions. Since the boys were all restless under their worry, and, since there is a contagious element in seeking a trouble-zone, none save Happy Jack, who was "sore" at them, and Weary stayed behind in the coulee with old Patsy while the others rode away up the grade and out toward Antelope coulee beyond.

They meant only to reconnoiter, and to warn the herders against attempting to cross Flying U coulee; though they were not exactly sure that they would be perfectly polite, or that they would confine themselves rigidly to the language they were wont to employ at dances. Andy Green, in particular, seemed rather to look forward with pleasure to the meeting. Andy, by the way, had remained heartbrokenly passive during that whole week, because Weary had extracted from him a promise which Andy, mendacious though he had the name of being, felt constrained to keep intact. Though of a truth it irked him much to think of two sheepherders walking abroad unpunished for their outrage upon his person.

Weary, as he had made plain to them all, wanted to avoid trouble if it were possible to do so. And, though they grinned together in secret over his own affair with Dunk—which was not, in their opinion, exactly pacific—they meant to respect his wishes as far as human nature was able to do so. So that the Happy Family, galloping toward the red sunset and the great, gray blot on the prairie, just where the glory of the west tinged the grass blades with red, were not one-half as blood-thirsty as they had proclaimed themselves to be.

While they were yet afar off they could see two men walking slowly in the immediate vicinity of the huddled band. A hundred yards away was a small tent, with a couple of horses picketed near by and feeding placidly. The men turned, gazed long at their approach, and walked to the tent, which they entered somewhat hastily.

"Look at 'em dodge outa sight, will you!" cried Cal Emmett, and lifted up his voice in the yell which sometimes announced the Happy Family's arrival in Dry Lake after a long, thirsty absence on roundup. Other voices joined in after that first, shrill "Ow-ow-ow-eee!" of Cal's; so that presently the whole lot of them were emitting nerve-crimping yells and spurring their horses into a thunder of hoofbeats, as they bore down upon the tent. Between howls they laughed, picturing to themselves four terrified sheepherders cowering within those frail, canvas walls.

"I'm a rambler, and a gambler, and far from my ho-o-me, And if yuh don't like me, jest leave me alo-o-ne!" chanted Big Medicine most horribly, and finished with a yell that almost scared himself and set his horse to plunging wildly.

"Come out of there, you lop-eared mutton-chewers, and let us pick the wool outa your teeth!" shouted Andy Green, telling himself hastily that this was not breaking his promise to Weary, and yielding to the temptation of coming as close to the guilty persons as he might; for, while these were not the men who had tied him and left him alone on the prairie, they belonged to the same outfit, and there was some comfort in giving them a few disagreeable minutes.

Pink, in the lead, was turning to ride around the tent, still yelling, when someone within the tent fired a rifle—and did not aim as high as he should. The bullet zipped close over the head of Big Medicine, who happened to be opposite the crack between the tent-flaps. The hand of Big Medicine jerked back to his hip; but, quick as he was, the Native Son plunged between him and the tent before he could take aim.

"Steady, amigo," smiled Miguel. "You aren't a crazy sheepherder."

"No, but I'm goin' to kill off one. Git outa my way!" Big Medicine was transformed into a cold-eyed, iron-jawed fighting machine. He dug the spurs in, meaning to ride ahead of Miguel. But Miguel's spurs also pressed home, so that the two horses plunged as one. Big Medicine, bellowing one solitary oath, drew his right leg from the stirrup to dismount. Miguel reached out, caught him by the arm, and held him to the saddle. And, though Big Medicine was a strong man, the grip held firm and unyielding.

"You must think of the outfit, you know," said Miguel, smiling still. "There must be no shooting. Once that begins—" He shrugged his shoulders with that slight, eloquent movement, which the Happy Family had come to know so well. He was speaking to them all, as they crowded up to the scuffle. "The man who feels the trigger-itch had better throw his gun away," he advised coolly. "I know, boys. I've seen these things start before. All hell can't stop you, once you begin to shoot. Put it up, Bud, or give it to me."

"The man don't live that can shoot at me, by cripes, and git away with it. Not if he misses killin' me!" Big Medicine was shaking with rage; but the Native Son saw that he hesitated, nevertheless, and laughed outright.

"Call him out and give him a thumping. That's good enough for a sheepherder," he suggested as a substitute.

Perhaps because the Native Son so seldom offered advice, and, because of his cool courage in interfering with Big Medicine at such a time, Bud's jaw relaxed and his pale eyes became more human in their expression. He even permitted Miguel to remove the big, wicked Colt from his hand, and slide it into his own pocket; whereat the Happy Family gasped with astonishment. Not even Pink would have dreamed of attempting such a thing.

"Well he's got to come out and take a lickin', anyway," shouted Big Medicine vengefully, and rode close enough to slap the canvas smartly with his quirt. By all the gods he knew by name he called upon the offender to come forth, while the others drew up in a rude half-circle to await developments. Heavy silence was the reply he got. It was as though the men within were sitting tense and watchful, like cougars crouched for a spring, with claws unsheathed and muscles quivering.

"You better come out," called Andy sharply, after they had waited a decent interval. "We didn't come here hunting trouble; we want to know where you're headed for with these sheep. The fellow that cut loose with the gun—"

"Aw, don't talk so purty! I'm gitting almighty tired, just setting here lettin' m' legs hang down. Git your ropes, boys!" With one sweeping gesture of his arm Big Medicine made plain his meaning as he rode a few paces away, his fingers fumbling with the string that held his rope. "I'm goin' to have a look at 'em, anyway," he grinned. "I sure do hate to see men act so bashful."

With his rope free and ready for action, Big Medicine shook the loop out, glanced around, and saw that Andy, Pink and Cal Emmett were also ready, and, with a dexterous flip, settled the noose neatly over the iron pin that thrust up through the end of the ridge-pole in front. Andy's loop sank neatly over it a second later, and the two wheeled and dashed away together, with Pink and Irish duplicating their performance at the other end of the tent. The dingy, smoke-stained canvas swayed, toppled, as the pegs gave way, and finally lay flat upon the prairie fifty feet from where it had stood, leaving the inmates exposed to the cruel stare of eight unfriendly cowpunchers. Four cowering figures they were, with guns in their hands that shook.

"Drop them guns!" thundered Big Medicine, flipping his rope loose and recoiling it mechanically as he plunged up to the group.

One man obeyed. One gave a squawk of terror and permitted his gun to go off at random before he fled toward the coulee. The other two crouched behind their bed-rolls, set their jaws doggedly and glared defiance.

Pink, Andy, Irish, Big Medicine and the Native Son slid off their horses and made a rush at them. A rifle barked viciously, and Slim, sitting prudently on his horse well in the rear, gave a yell and started for home at a rapid pace.

Considering the provocation the Happy Family behaved with quite praiseworthy self-control and leniency. They did not lynch those two herders. They did not kill them, either by bullets, knives, or beating to death. They took away the guns, however, and they told them with extreme bluntness what sort of men they believed them to be. They defined accurately their position in society at large, in that neighborhood, and stated what would be their future fate if they persisted in acting with so little caution and common sense.

At Andy Green's earnest behest they also wound them round and round with ropes, before they departed, and gave them some very good advice upon the matter of range rules and the herding of sheep, particularly of Dot sheep.

"You're playing big luck, if you only had sense enough to know it," Andy pointed out to the recumbent three before they rode away. "We didn't come over here on the warpath, and, if you hadn't got in such a darned hurry to start something, you'd be a whole lot more comfortable right now. We rode over to tell yuh not to start them sheep across Flying U coulee; because, if you do, you're going to have both hands and your hats plumb full uh trouble. It has taken some little time and fussing to get yuh gentled down so we can talk to you, and I sure do hope yuh remember what I'm saying."

"Oh, we'll remember it, all right!" menaced one of the men, lifting his head turtlewise that he might glare at the group. "And our bosses'll remember it; you needn't worry about that none. You wait till—"

The next man to him turned his head and muttered a sentence, and the speaker dropped his head back upon the ground, silenced.

"It was your own outfit started this style of rope trimming, so you can't kick about that part of the deal," Pink informed them melodiously. "It's liable to get to be all the rage with us. So, if you don't like it, don't come around where we are. And say!" His dimples stood deep in his cheeks. "You send those ropes home to-morrow, will yuh? We're liable to need 'em."

"By cripes!" Big Medicine bawled. "What say we haze them sheep a few miles north, boys?"

"Oh, I guess they'll be all right where they are," Andy protested, his thirst for revenge assuaged at sight of those three trussed as he had been trussed, and apparently not liking it any better than he had liked it. "They'll be good and careful not to come around the Flying U—or I miss my guess a mile."

The others cast comprehensive glances at their immediate surroundings, and decided that they had at least made their meaning plain; there was no occasion for emphasizing their disapproval any further. They confiscated the rifles, and they told the fellows why they did so. They very kindly pulled a tarpaulin over the three to protect them in a measure from the chill night that was close upon them, and they wished them good night and pleasant dreams, and rode away home.

On the way they met Weary and Happy Jack, galloping anxiously to the battle scene. Slim, it appeared from Weary's rapid explanation, had arrived at the ranch with his horse in a lather and with a four-inch furrow in the fleshiest part of his leg, where a bullet had flicked him in passing. The tale he told had led Weary to believe that Slim was the sole survivor of that reckless company.

"Mamma! I'm so glad to see you boys able to fork your horses and swear natural, that I don't believe I can speak my little piece about staying on your own side the fence and letting trouble do some of the hunting," he exclaimed thankfully. "I wish you'd stayed at home and left these blamed Dots alone. But, seeing yuh didn't, I'm tickled to death to hear you didn't kill anybody off. I don't want the folks to come home and find the whole bunch in the pen. It might look as if—"

"You don't want the folks to come home and find the whole ranch sheeped off, either, and the herders camping up in the white house, do yuh?" Pink inquired pointedly. "I kinda think," he added dryly, "those same herders will feel like going away around Flying U fences with their sheep. I don't believe they'll do any cutting across."

"I betche old Dunk'll make it interestin' fer this outfit, just the same," Happy Jack predicted. "Tyin' up three men uh hisn, like that, and ropin' their tent and draggin' it off, ain't things he'll pass up. He'll have a possy out here—you see if he don't!"

"In that case, I'll be sorry for you, Happy," purred Miguel close beside him. "You're the only one in the outfit that looks capable of such a vile deed."

"Oh, Dunk won't do anything," Weary said cheerfully. "You'll have to take those guns back, though. They might take a notion to call that stealing!"

"You forget," the Native Son reminded calmly, "that we left them three good ropes in exchange."

Whereupon the Happy Family laughed and went to offer their unsought sympathy to Slim.

CHAPTER X. The Happy Family Herd Sheep

The boys of the Flying U had many faults in common, aside from certain individual frailties; one of their chief weaknesses was over-confidence in their own ability to cope with any situation which might arise, unexpectedly or otherwise, and a belief that others felt that same confidence in them, and that enemies were wont to sit a long time counting the cost before venturing to offer too great an affront. Also they believed—and made it manifest in their conversation—that they could even bring the Old Man back to health if they only had him on the ranch where they could get at him. They maligned the hospitals and Chicago doctors most unjustly, and were agreed that all he needed was to be back on the ranch where somebody could look after him right. They asserted that, if they ever got tired of living and wanted to cash in without using a gun or anything, they'd go to a hospital and tell the doctors to turn loose and try to cure them of something.

This by way of illustration; also as an explanation of their sleeping soundly that night, instead of watching for some hostile demonstration on the part of the Dot outfit. To a man—one never counted Happy Jack's prophecies of disaster as being anything more than a personal deformity of thought—they were positive in their belief that the Dot sheepherders would be very, very careful not to provoke the Happy Family to further manifestations of disapproval. They knew what they'd get, if they tried any more funny business, and they'd be mighty careful where they drove their sheep after this.

So, with the comfortable glow of victory in their souls, they laid them down, and, when the animated discussion of that night's adventure flagged, as their tongues grew sleep-clogged and their eyelids drooped, they slept in peace; save when Slim, awakened by the soreness of his leg, grunted a malediction or two before he began snoring again.

71

They rose and ate their breakfast in a fair humor with the world. One grows accustomed to the thought of sickness, even when it strikes close to the affections, and, with the resilience of youth and hope, life adjusts itself to make room for the specter of fear, so that it does not crowd unduly, but stands half-forgotten in the background of one's thoughts. For that reason they no longer spoke soberly because of the Old Man lying hurt unto death in Chicago. And, when they mentioned the Dot sheep and men, they spoke as men speak of the vanquished.

With the taste of hot biscuits and maple syrup still lingering pleasantly against their palates, they went out and were confronted with sheep, blatting sheep, stinking sheep, devastating sheep, Dot sheep. On the south side of the coulee, up on the bluff, grazed the band. They fed upon the brow of the hill opposite the ranch buildings; they squeezed under the fence and spilled a ragged fringe of running, gray animals down the slope. Half a mile away though the nearest of them were, the murmur of them, the smell of them, the whole intolerable presence of them, filled the Happy Family with an amazed loathing too deep for words.

Technically, that high, level stretch of land bounding Flying U coulee on the south was open range. It belonged to the government. The soil was not fertile enough even for the most optimistic of "dry land" farmers to locate upon it; and this was before the dry-land farming craze had swept the country, gathering in all public land as claims. J. G. Whitmore had contented himself with acquiring title to the whole of the Flying U coulee, secure in his belief that the old order of things would not change, in his life-time, at least, and that the unwritten law of the range land, which leaves the vicinity of a ranch to the use of the ranch owner, would never be repealed by new customs imposed by a new class of people.

Legally, there was no trespassing of the Dots, beyond the two or three hundred which had made their way through the fence. Morally, however, and by right of custom, their offense would not be much greater if they came on down the hill and invaded the Old Man's pet meadows, just beyond the "little pasture."

Ladies may read this story, so I am not going to pretend to repeat the things they said, once they were released from dumb amazement. I should be compelled to improvise and substitute—which would remove much of the flavor. Let bare facts suffice, at present.

They saddled in haste, and in haste they rode to the scene. This, they were convinced, was the band herded by the bug-killer and the man from Wyoming; and the nerve of those two almost excited the admiration of the Happy Family. It did not, however, deter them from their purpose.

Weary, to look at him, was no longer in the mood to preach patience and a turning of the other cheek. He also made that change of heart manifest in his speech when Pink, his eyes almost black, rode up close and gritted at him:

"Well, what's the orders now? Want me to go back and get the wire nippers so we can let them poor little sheep down into the meadow? Maybe we better ask the herders down to have some of Patsy's grub, too; I don't believe they had time to cook much breakfast. And it wouldn't be a bad idea to haze our own stuff clear off the range. I'm afraid Dunk's sheep are going to fare kinda slim, if we go on letting our cattle eat all the good grass!" Pink did not often indulge in such lengthy sarcasm, especially toward his beloved Weary; but his exasperation toward Weary's mild tactics had been growing apace.

Weary's reply, I fear, will have to be omitted. It was terribly unrefined.

"I want you boys to spread out, around the whole bunch," was his first printable utterance, "and haze these sheep just as far south as they can get without taking to the river. Don't get all het up chasing 'em yourself—make the men (Weary did not call them men; he called them something very naughty) that's paid for it do the driving."

"And, if they don't go," drawled the smooth voice of the Native Son, "what shall we do, amigo? Slap them on the wrist?"

Weary twisted in the saddle and sent him a baleful glance, which was not at all like Weary the sunny-hearted.

"If you can't figure that out for yourself," he snapped, "you had better go back and wipe the dishes for Patsy; and, when that's done, you can pull the weeds out of his radishes. Maybe he'll give you a nickel to buy candy with, if you do it good." Before he faced to the front again his harsh glance swept the faces of his companions.

They were grinning, every man of them, and he knew why. To see him lose his temper was something of an event with the Happy Family, who used sometimes to fix the date of an incident by saying, "It was right after that time Weary got mad, a year ago last fall," or something of the sort. He grinned himself, shamefacedly, and told them that they were a bunch of no-account cusses, anyway, and he'd just about as soon herd sheep himself as to have to run with such an outfit; which swept his anger from him and left him his usual self, with but the addition of a purpose from which nothing could stay him. He was going to settle the sheep question, and he was going to settle it that day.

Only one injunction did he lay upon the Happy Family. "You fellows don't want to get excited and go to shooting," he warned, while they were still out of hearing of the herders. "We don't want Dunk to get anything like that on us; savvy?"

They "savvied," and they told him so, each after his own individual manner.

"I guess we ought to be able to put the run on a couple of sheepherders, without wasting any powder," Pink said loftily, remembering his meeting with them a few days before.

"One thing sure—we'll make a good job of it this time," promised Irish, and spurred after Weary, who was leading the way around the band.

The herders watched them openly and with the manner of men who are expecting the worst to happen. Unlike the four whose camp had been laid low the night before, these two were unarmed, as they had been from the first; which, in Weary's opinion, was a bit of guile upon the part of Dunk. If trouble came—trouble which it would take a jury to settle—the fact that the sheepmen were unarmed would tell heavily in their favor; for, while the petty meanness of range-stealing and nagging trespass may be harder to bear than the flourishing of a gun before one's face, it all sounds harmless enough in the telling.

Weary headed straight for the nearest herder, told him to put his dogs to work rounding up the sheep, which were scattered over an area half a mile across while they fed, and, when the herder, who was the bug-killer, made no move to obey, Weary deliberately pulled his gun and pointed at his head.

"You move," he directed with grim intent, "and don't take too much time about it, either."

The bug-killer, an unkempt, ungainly figure, standing with his back to the morning sun, scowled up at Weary stolidly.

"Yuh dassent shoot," he stated sourly, and did not move.

For answer, Weary pulled back the hammer; also he smiled as malignantly as it was in his nature to do, and hoped in his heart that he looked sufficiently terrifying to convince the man. So they faced each other in a silent clash of wills.

Big Medicine had not been saying much on the way over, which was unusual. Now he rode forward until he was abreast of Weary, and he grinned down at the bug-killer in a way to distract his attention from the gun.

"Nobody don't have to shoot, by cripes!" he bawled. "We hain't goin' to kill yuh. We'll make yuh wisht, by cripes, we had, though, b'fore we git through. Git to work, boys, 'n' gether up some dry grass an' sticks. Over there in them rose-bushes you oughta find enough bresh. We'll give him a taste uh what we was talkin' about comm' over, by cripes! I guess he'll be willin' to drive sheep, all right, when we git through with him. Haw-haw-haw-w-w!" He leaned forward in the saddle and ogled the bug-killer with horrid significance.

"Git busy with that bresh!" he yelled authoritatively, when a glance showed him that the Happy Family was hesitating and eyeing him uncertainly. "Git a fire goin' quick's yuh kin—I'll do the rest. Down in Coconino county we used to have a way uh fixin' sheepherders—"

"Aw, gwan! We don't want no torture business!" remonstrated Happy Jack uneasily, edging away.

"Yuh don't, hey?" Big Medicine turned in the saddle wrathfully and glared. When he had succeeded in catching Andy Green's eye he winked, and that young man's face kindled understandingly. "Well, now, you hain't runnin' this here show. Honest to grandma, I've saw the time when a little foot-warmin' done a sheepherder a whole lot uh good; and, it looks to me, by cripes, as if this here feller needed a dose to gentle him down. You git the fire started. That's all I want you t' do, Happy. Some uh you boys help me rope him—like him and that other jasper over there done to Andy. C'mon, Andy—it ain't goin' to take long!"

"You bet your sweet life I'll come on!" exclaimed Andy, dismounting eagerly. "Let me take your rope, Weary. Too bad we haven't got a branding iron—"

"Aw, we don't need no irons." Big Medicine was also on the ground by then, and untying his rope. "Lemme git his shoes off once, and I'll show yuh."

The bug-killer lifted his stick, snarling like a mongrel dog when a stranger tries to drive it out of the house; hurled the stick hysterically, as Big Medicine, rope in hand, advanced implacably, and, with a squawk of horror, turned suddenly and ran. After him, bellowing terribly, lunged Big Medicine, straight through the band like a snowplow, leaving behind them a wide, open trail.

"Say, we kinda overplayed that bet, by gracious," Andy commented to Weary, while he watched the chase. "That gazabo's scared silly; let's try the other one. That torture talk works fine."

In his enthusiasm Andy remounted and was about to lead the way to the other herder when Big Medicine returned puffing, the bug-killer squirming in his grasp. "Tell him what yuh want him to do, Weary," he panted, with some difficulty holding his limp victim upright by a greasy coat-collar. "And if he don't fall over himself doin' it, why—by cripes— we'll take off his shoes!"

Whereupon the bug-killer gave another howl and professed himself eager to drive the sheep—well, what he said was that he would drive them to that place which ladies dislike to hear mentioned, if the Happy Family wanted him to.

"That's all right, then. Start 'em south, and don't quit till somebody tells you to." Weary carefully let down the hammer of his six-shooter and shoved it thankfully into his scabbard.

"Now, you don't want to pile it on quite so thick, next time," Irish admonished Big Medicine, when they turned away from watching the bug-killer set his dogs to work by gestures and a shouted word or two. "You like to have sent this one plumb nutty."

"I betche Bud gets us all pinched for that," grumbled Happy Jack. "Torturing folks is purty darned serious business. You might as well shoot 'em up decent and be done with it."

"Haw-haw-haw-w-w!" Big Medicine ogled the group mirthfully. "Nobody can't swear I done a thing, or said a thing. All I said definite was that I'd take off his shoes. Any jury in the country'd know that would be hull lot worse fer us than it would fer him, by cripes. Haw-haw-haw-w-w!"

"Say, that's right; yuh didn't say nothin', ner do nothin'. By golly, that was purty slick work, all right!" Slim forgot his sore leg until he clapped his hand enthusiastically down upon the place as comprehension of Bud's finesse dawned upon him. He yelped, and the Happy Family laughed unfeelingly.

"You want to be careful and don't try to see through any jokes, Slim, till that leg uh yours gets well," Irish bantered, and they laughed the louder.

All this was mere byplay; a momentary swinging of their mood to pleasantry, because they were a temperamentally cheerful lot, and laughter came to them easily, as it always does to youth and perfect mental and physical health. Their brief hilarity over Slim's misfortune did not swerve them from their purpose, nor soften the mood of them toward their adversaries. They were unsmiling and unfriendly when they reached the man from Wyoming; and, if they ever behaved like boys let out of school, they did not show it then.

The Wyoming man was wiser than his fellow. He had been given several minutes grace in which to meditate upon the unwisdom of defiance; and he had seen the bug-killer change abruptly from sullenness to terror, and afterward to abject obedience. He did not know what they had said to him, or what they had done; but he knew the bug-killer was a hard man to stampede. And he was one man, and they were many; also he judged that, being human, and this being the third offense of the Dot sheep under his care, it would be extremely unsafe to trust that their indignation would vent itself in mere words.

Therefore, when Weary told him to get the stragglers back through the fence and up on the level, he stopped only long enough for a good look at their faces. After that he called his dogs and crawled through the fence.

It really did not require the entire Family to force those sheep south that morning. But Weary's jaw was set, as was his heart, upon a thorough cleaning of that particular bit of range; and, since he did not definitely request any man to turn back, and every fellow there was minded to see the thing to a finish, they straggled out behind the trailing two thousand—and never had one bunch of sheep so efficient a convoy.

After the first few miles the way grew rough. Sheep lagged, and the blatting increased to an uproar. Old ewes and yearlings these were mostly, and there were few to suffer more than hunger and thirst, perhaps. So Weary was merciless, and drove them forward without a stop until the first jumble of hills and deep-worn gullies held them back from easy traveling.

But the Happy Family had not ridden those breaks for cattle, all these years, to be hindered by rough going. Weary, when the band stopped and huddled, blatting incessantly against a sheer wall of sandstone and gravel, got the herders together and told them what he wanted.

"You take 'em down that slope till you come to the second little coulee. Don't go up the first one—that's a blind pocket. In the second coulee, up a mile or so, there's a spring creek. You can hold 'em there on water for half an hour. That's more than any of yuh deserve. Haze 'em down there."

The herders did not know it, but that second coulee was the rude gateway to an intricate system of high ridges and winding waterways that would later be dry as a bleached bone—the real beginning of the bad lands which border the Missouri river for long, terrible miles. Down there, it is possible for two men to reach places where they may converse quite easily across a chasm, and yet be compelled to ride fifteen or twenty miles, perhaps, in order to shake hands. Yet, even in that scrap-heap of Nature there are ways of passing deep into the heart of the upheaval.

The Happy Family knew those ways as they knew the most complicated figures of the quadrilles they danced so lightfootedly with the girls of the Bear Paw country. When they forced the sheep and their herders out of the coulee Weary had indicated he sent Irish and Pink ahead to point the way, and he told them to head for the Wash Bowl; which they did with praiseworthy zeal and scant pity for the sheep.

When at last, after a slow, heartbreaking climb up a long, bare ridge, Pink and Irish paused upon the brow of a slope and let the trail-weary band spill itself reluctantly down the steep slope beyond, the sun stood high in the blue above them and their stomachs clamored for food; by which signs they knew that it must be near noon.

When the last sheep had passed, blatting discordantly, down the bluff, Weary halted the sweating herders for a parting admonition.

"We don't aim to deal you any more misery, for a while, if you stay where you're at. You're only working for a living, like the rest of us— but I must say I don't admire your trade none. Anyway, I'll send some of your bunch down here with grub and beds. This is good enough range for sheep. You keep away from the Flying U and nobody'll bother you. Over there in them trees," he added, pointing a gloved finger toward a little grove on the far side of the basin, "you'll find a cabin, and water. And, farther down the river there's pretty good grass, in the little bottoms. Now, git."

The herders looked as if they would enjoy murdering them all, but they did not say a word. With their dogs at heel they scrambled down the bluff in the wake of their sheep, and the Happy Family, rolling cigarettes while they watched them depart, told one another that this settled that bunch; they wouldn't bed down in the Flying U door-yard that night, anyway.

CHAPTER XI. Weary Unburdens

Hungry with the sharp, gnawing hunger of healthy stomachs accustomed to regular and generous feeding; tired with the weariness of healthy muscles pushed past their accustomed limit of action; and hot with the unaccustomed heat of a blazing day shunted unaccountably into the midst of soft spring weather, the Happy Family rode out of the embrace of the last barren coulee and up on the wide level where the breeze swept gratefully up from the west, and where every day brought with it a deeper tinge of green into its grassy carpet.

Only for this harassment of the Dot sheep, the roundup wagons would be loaded and ready to rattle abroad over the land. Meadow larks and curlews and little, pert-eyed ground sparrows called out to them that roundup time was come. They passed a bunch of feeding Flying U cattle, and flat-ribbed, bandy-legged calves galloped in brief panic to their mothers and from the sanctuary of grass-filled paunches watched the riders with wide, inquisitive eyes.

"We ought to be starting out, by now," Weary observed a bit gloomily to Andy and Pink, who rode upon either side of him. "The calf crop is going to be good, if this weather holds on another two weeks or so. But—" he waved his cigarette disgustedly "—that darned Dot outfit would be all over the place, if we pulled out on roundup and left 'em the run of things." He smoked moodily for a minute. "My religion has changed a lot in the last few days," he observed whimsically. "My idea of hell is a place where there ain't anything but sheep and sheepherders; and cowpunchers have got to spend thousands uh years right in the middle of the corrals."

"If that's the case, I'm going to quit cussing, and say my prayers every night," Andy Green asserted emphatically.

"What worries me," Weary confided, obeying the impulse to talk over his troubles with those who sympathized, "is how I'm going to keep the work going along like it ought to, and at the same time keep them Dot sheep outa the house. Dunk's wise, all right. He knows enough about the cow business to know we ye got to get out on the range pretty quick, now. And he's so mean that every day or every half day he can feed his sheep on Flying U grass, he calls that much to the good. And he knows we won't go to opening up any real gun-fights if we can get out of it; he counts on our faunching around and kicking up a lot of dust, maybe— but we won't do anything like what he'd do, in our places. He knows the Old Man and Chip are gone, and he knows we've just naturally got to sit back and swallow our tongues because we haven't any authority. Mamma! It comes pretty tough, when a low-down skunk like that just banks on your doing the square thing. He wouldn't do it, but he knows we will; and so he takes advantage of white men and gets the best of 'em. And if we should happen to break out and do something, he knows the herders would be the ones to get it in the neck; and he'd wait till the dust settled, and bob up with the sheriff—" He waved his hand again with a hopeless gesture. "It may not look that way on the face of it," he added gloomily, "but Dunk has got us right where he wants us. From the way they've been letting sheep on our land, time and time again, I'd gamble he's just trying to make us so mad we'll break out. He's got it in for the whole outfit, from the Old Man and the Little Doctor down to Slim. If any of us boys got into trouble, the Old Man would spend his last cent to clear us; and Dunk knows that just as well as he knows the way from the house to the stable. He'd see to it that it would just about take the Old Man's last cent, too. And he's using these Dot sheep like you'd use a red flag on a bull, to make us so crazy mad we'll kill off somebody.

"That's why," he said to them all when he saw that they had ridden up close that they might hear what he was saying, "I've been hollering so loud for the meek-and-mild stunt. When I slapped him on the jaw, and he stood there and took it, I saw his game. He had a witness to swear I hit him and he didn't hit back. And when I saw them Dots in our field again, I knew, just as well as if Dunk had told me, that he was kinda hoping we'd kill a herder or two so he could cinch us good and plenty. I don't say," he qualified with a rueful grin, "that Dunk went into the sheep business just to get r-re-venge, as they say in shows. But if he can make money running sheep—and he can, all right, because there's more money in them right now than there is in cattle—and at the same time get a good whack at the Flying U, he's the lad that will sure make a running jump at the chance." He spat upon the burnt end of his cigarette stub from force of the habit that fear of range fires had built, and cast it petulantly from him; as if he would like to have been able to throw Dunk and his sheep problem as easily out of his path.

"So I wish you boys would hang onto yourselves when you hear a sheep blatting under your window," he summed up his unburdening whimsically. "As Bud said this morning, you can't hang a man for telling a sheepherder you'll take off his shoes. And they can't send us over the road for moving that band of sheep onto new range to-day. Last night you all were kinda disorderly, maybe, but you didn't hurt anybody, or destroy any property. You see what I mean. Our only show is to stop with our toes on the right side of the dead line."

"If Andy, here, would jest git his think-wheels greased and going good," Big Medicine suggested loudly, "he ought to frame up something that would put them Dots on the run permanent. I d'no, by cripes, why it is a feller can always think uh lies and joshes by the dozens, and put 'em over O. K. when there ain't nothing to be made out of it except hard feelin's; and then when a deal like this here sheep deal comes up, he's got about as many idees, by cripes, as that there line-back calf over there. Honest to grandma, Andy makes me feel kinda faint. Only time he did have a chanc't, he let them—" It occurred to Big Medicine at that point that perhaps his remarks might be construed by the object of them as being offensively personal. He turned his head and grinned good-naturedly in Andy's direction, and refrained from finishing what he was going to say. "I sure do like them wind-flowers scattered all over the ground," he observed with such deliberate and ostentatious irrelevance that the Happy Family laughed, even to Andy Green, who had at first been inclined toward anger.

"Everything," declared Andy in the tone of a paid instructor, "has its proper time and place, boys; I've told you that before. For instance, I wouldn't try to kill a skunk by talking it to death; and I wouldn't be hopeful of putting the run on this Dunk person by telling him ghost stories. As to ideas—I'm plumb full of them. But they're all about grub, just right at present."

That started Slim and Happy Jack to complaining because no one had had sense enough to go back after some lunch before taking that long trail south; the longer because it was a slow one, with sheep to set the pace. And by the time they had presented their arguments against the Happy Family's having enough brains to last them overnight, and the Happy Family had indignantly pointed out just where the mental deficiency was most noticeable, they were upon that last, broad stretch of "bench" land beyond which lay Flying U coulee and Patsy and dinner; a belated dinner, to be sure, but for that the more welcome.

And when they reached the point where they could look away to the very rim of the coulee, they saw sheep—sheep to the skyline, feeding scattered and at ease, making the prairie look, in the distance, as if it were covered with a thin growth of gray sage-brush. Four herders moved slowly upon the outskirts, and the dogs were little, scurrying, black dots which stopped occasionally to wait thankfully until the master-minds again urged them to endeavor.

The Happy Family drew up and stared in silence.

"Do I see sheep?" Pink inquired plaintively at last. "Tell me, somebody."

"It's that bunch you fellows tackled last night," said Weary miserably. "I ought to have had sense enough to leave somebody on the ranch to look out for this."

"They've got their nerve," stated Irish, "after the deal they got last night. I'd have bet good money that you couldn't drag them herders across Flying U coulee with a log chain."

"Say, by golly, do we have to drive this here bunch anywheres before we git anything to eat?" Slim wanted to know distressfully.

Weary considered briefly. "No, I guess we'll pass 'em up for the present. An hour or so won't make much difference in the long run, and our horses are about all in, right now—"

"So'm I, by cripes!" Big Medicine attested, grinning mirthlessly. "This here sheep business is plumb wearin' on a man. 'Specially," he added with a fretful note, "when you've got to handle 'em gentle. The things I'd like to do to them Dots is all ruled outa the game, seems like. Honest to grandma, a little gore would look better to me right now than a Dutch picnic before the foam's all blowed off the refreshments. Lemme kill off jest one herder, Weary?" he pleaded. "The one that took a shot at me las' night. Purty, please!"

"If you killed one," Weary told him glumly, "you might as well make a clean sweep and take in the whole bunch."

"Well, I won't charge nothin' extra fer that, either," Bud assured him generously. "I'm willin' to throw in the other three—and the dawgs, too, by cripes!" He goggled the Happy Family quizzically. "Nobody can't say there's anything small about me. Why, down in the Coconino country they used to set half a dozen greasers diggin' graves, by cripes, soon as I started in to argy with a man. It was a safe bet they'd need three or four, anyways, if old Bud cut loose oncet. Sheepherders? Why, they jest natcherly couldn't keep enough on hand, securely, to run their sheep. They used to order sheepherders like they did woolsacks, by cripes! You could always tell when I was in the country, by the number uh extra herders them sheep outfits always kep' in reserve. Honest to grandma, I've knowed two or three outfits to club together and ship in a carload at a time, when they heard I was headed their way. And so when it comes to killin' off four, why that ain't skurcely enough to make it worth m'while to dirty up m'gun!"

"Aw, I betche yuh never killed a man in your life!" Happy Jack grumbled in his characteristic tone of disparagement; but such was his respect for Big Medicine's prowess that he took care not to speak loud enough to be overheard by that modest gentleman, who continued with certain fearsome details of alleged murderous exploits of his own, down in Coconino County, Arizona.

But as they passed the detested animals, thankful that the trail permitted them to ride by at a distance sufficient to blur the most unsavory details, even Big Medicine gave over his deliberate boastings and relapsed into silence.

He had begun his fantastic vauntings from an instinctive impulse to leaven with humor a situation which, at the moment, could not be bettered. Just as they had, when came the news of the Old Man's dire plight, sought to push the tragedy of it into the background and cling to their creed of optimism, they had avoided openly facing the sheep complication squarely with mutual admissions of all it might mean to the Flying U.

Until Weary had unburdened his heart of worry on the ride home that day, they had not said much about it, beyond a general vilification of the sheep industry as a whole, of Dunk as the chief of the encroaching Dots, and of the herders personally.

But there were times when they could not well avoid thinking rather deeply upon the subject, even if they did refuse to put their forebodings into speech. They were not children; neither were they to any degree lacking in intelligence. Swearing, about herders and at them, was all very well; bluffing, threatening, pummeling even with willing fists, tearing down tents and binding men with ropes might serve to relieve the emotions upon occasion. But there was the grim economic problem which faced squarely the Flying U as a "cow outfit"—the problem of range and water; the Happy Family did not call it by name, but they realized to the full what it meant to the Old Man to have sheep just over his boundary line always. They realized, too, what it meant to have the Old Man absent at this time—worse, to have him lying in a hospital, likely to die at any moment; what it meant to have the whole responsibility shifted to their shoulders, willing though they might be to bear the burden; what it meant to have the general of an army gone when the enemy was approaching in overwhelming numbers.

Pink, when they were descending the first slope of the bluff which was the southern rim of Flying U coulee, turned and glared vindictively back at the wavering, gray blanket out there to the west. When he faced to the front his face had the look it wore when he was fighting.

"So help me, Josephine!" he gritted desperately, "we've got to clean the range of them Dots before the Old Man comes back, or—" He snapped his jaws shut viciously.

Weary turned haggard eyes toward him.

"How?" he asked simply. And Pink had no answer for him.

CHAPTER XII. Two of a Kind

Patsy, staunch old partisan that he was, placed before them much food which he had tried his best to keep hot without burning everything to a crisp, and while they ate with ravenous haste he told, with German epithets and a trembling lower jaw, of his troubles that day.

"Dem sheeps, dey coom by der leetle pasture," he lamented while he poured coffee muddy from long boiling. "Looks like dey know so soon you ride away, und dey cooms cheeky as you pleece, und eats der grass und crawls under der fence and leafs der vool sthicking by der vires. I goes out mit a club, py cosh, und der sheeps chust looks und valks by some better place alreatty, und I throw rocks and yells till mine neck iss sore.

"Und' dose herders, dey sets dem by der rock and laugh till I felt like I could kill der whole punch, by cosh! Und von yells, 'Hey, dutchy, pring me some pie, alreatty!' Und he laughs some more pecause der sheeps dey don't go avay; dey chust run around und eat more grass and baa-aa!" He turned and went heavily back to the greasy range with the depleted coffee pot, lifted the lid of a kettle and looked in upon the contents with a purely mechanical glance; gave a perfunctory prod or two with a long-handled fork, and came back to stand uneasily behind Weary.

"If you poys are goin' to shtand fer dot," he began querulously, "Py cosh I von't! Py myself I vill go and tell dot Dunk W'ittaker vot lowdown skunk I t'ink he iss. Sheep's vool shtickin' by der fences efferwhere on der ranch, py cosh! Dot vould sure kill der Old Man quick if he see it. Shtinkin' off sheeps py our noses all der time, till I can't eat no more mit der shmell of dem. Neffer pefore did I see vool on der Flying U fences, py cosh, und sheeps baa-aain' in der coulee!"

Never had they seen Patsy take so to heart a matter of mere business importance. They did not say much to him; there was not much that they could say. They ate their fill and went out disconsolately to discuss the thing among themselves, away from Patsy's throaty complainings. They hated it as badly as did he; with Weary's urgent plea for no violence holding them in leash, they hated it more, if that were possible.

The Native Son tilted his head unobtrusively stableward when he caught Andy's eye, and as unobtrusively wandered away from the group. Andy stopped long enough to roll and light a cigarette and then strolled after him with apparent aimlessness, secretly curious over the summons. He found Miguel in the stable waiting for him, and Miguel led the way, rope in hand across the corral and into the little pasture where fed a horse he meant to ride. He did not say anything until he had turned to close the gate, and to make sure that they were alone and that their departure had not carried to the Happy Family any betraying air of significance.

"You remember when you blew in here, a few weeks or so ago?" the Native Son asked abruptly, a twinkle in his fathomless eyes. "You put up a good one on the boys, that time, you remember. Bluffed them into thinking I was a hero in disguise, and that you'd seen me pull off a big stunt of bull-fighting and bull-dogging down in Mexico. It was a fine josh. They believe it yet."

Andy glanced at him perplexedly. "Yes—but when it turned out to be true," he amended, "the josh was on me, I guess; I thought I was just lying, when I wasn't. I've wondered a good deal about that. By gracious, it makes a man feel funny to frame up a yarn out of his own think-machine, and then find out he's been telling the truth all the while. It's like a fellow handing out a twenty-four karat gold bar to a rube by mistake, under the impression it only looks like one. Of course they believe it! Only they don't know I just merely hit the truth by accident."

The Native Son smiled his slow, amused smile, that somehow never failed to be impressive. "That's the funny part of it," he drawled. "You didn't. I just piled another little josh on top of yours, that's all. I never throwed a bull in my life, except with my lariat. I'd heard a good deal about you, and—well, I thought I'd see if I could go you one better. And you put that Mexico yarn across so smooth and easy, I just simply couldn't resist the temptation to make you think it was all straight goods. Sabe?"

Andy Green did not say a word, but he looked exceedingly foolish.

"So I think we can both safely consider ourselves top-hands when it comes to lying," the Native Son went on shamelessly. "And if you're willing to go in with me on it and help put Dunk on the run—" He glanced over his shoulder, saw that Happy Jack, on horseback, was coming out to haze in the saddle bunch, and turned to stroll back as lazily as he had come. He continued to speak smoothly and swiftly, in a voice that would not carry ten paces. While Andy Green, with brown head bent attentively, listened eagerly and added a sentence or two on his own account now and then, and smiled—which he had not been in the habit of doing lately.

"Say, you fellers are gittin' awful energetic, ain't yuh?—wranglin' horses afoot!" Happy Jack bantered at the top of his voice when he passed them by. "Better save up your strength while you kin. Weary's goin' to set us herdin' sheep agin—and I betche there's goin' to be something more'n herdin' on our hands before we git through."

"I wouldn't be a bit surprised if there was," sang out Andy, as cheerfully as if he had been invited to dance "Ladies' choice" with the prettiest girl in the crowd. "Wonder what hole he's going to dump this bunch into," he added to the Native Son. "By gracious, he ought to send 'em just as far north as he can drive 'em without paying duty! I'd sure take 'em over into Canada, if it was me running the show."

"It was a mistake," the Native Son volunteered, "for the whole bunch to go off like we did to-day. They had those sheep up here on the hill just for a bait. They knew we'd go straight up in the air and come down on those two freaks herding 'em, and that gave them the chance to cross the other bunch. I thought so all along, but I didn't like to butt in."

"Well Weary's mad enough now to do things that will leave a dent, anyway," Andy commented under his breath when, from the corral gate, he got a good look at Weary's profile, which showed the set of his mouth and chin. "See that mouth? It's hunt the top rail, and do it quick, when old Weary straightens out his lips like that."

Behind them, Happy Jack bellowed for an open gate and no obstructions, and they drew hastily to one side to let the saddle horses gallop past with a great upflinging of dust. Pink, with a quite obtrusive facetiousness, began lustily chanting that it looked to him like a big night to-night—with occasional, furtive glances at Weary's face; for he, also, had been quick to read those close-pressed lips, which did not soften in response to the ditty. Usually he laughed at Pink's drollery.

They rode rather quietly upon the hill again, to where fed the sheep. During the hour or so that they had been absent the sheep had not moved appreciably; they still grazed close enough to the boundary to make their position seem a direct insult to the Flying U, a virtual slap in the face. And these young men who worked for the Flying U, and who made its interests right loyally their own, were growing very, very tired of turning the other cheek. With them, the time for profanity and for horseplay bluffing and judicious temporizing was past. There were other lips besides Weary's that were drawn tight and thin when they approached that particular band of sheep. More than one pair of eyes turned inquiringly toward him and away again when they met no answering look.

They topped a rise of ground, and in the shallow wrinkle which had hidden him until now they came full upon Dunk Whittaker, riding a chunky black which stepped restlessly about while he conferred in low tones with a couple of the herders. The Happy Family recognized them as two of the fellows in whose safe keeping they had left their ropes the night before. Dunk looked around quickly when the group appeared over the little ridge, scowled, hesitated and then came straight up to them.

"I want you rowdies to bring back those sheep you took the trouble to drive off this morning," he began, with the even, grating voice and the sneering lift of lip under his little, black mustache which the older members of the Happy Family remembered—and hated—so vividly. "I've stood just all I'm going to stand, of these typically Flying U performances you've been indulging in so freely during the past week. It's all very well to terrorize a neighborhood of long-haired rubes who don't know enough to teach you your places; but interfering with another man's property is—"

"Interfering with another—what?" Big Medicine, his pale blue eyes standing out more like a frog's than ever upon his face, gave his horse a kick and lunged close that he might lean and thrust his red face near to Dunk's. "Another what? I don't see nothin' in your saddle that looks t'me like a man, by cripes! All I can see is a smooth-skinned, slippery vermin I'd hate to name a snake after, that crawls around in the dark and lets cheap rough-necks do all his dirty work. I've saw dogs sneak up and grab a man behind, but most always they let out a growl or two first. And even a rattler is square enough to buzz at yuh and give yuh a chanc't to side-step him. Honest to grandma, I don't hardly know what kinda reptyle y'are. I hate to insult any of 'em, by cripes, by namin' yuh after 'em. But don't, for Lordy's sake, ever call yourself a man agin!"

Big Medicine turned his head and spat disgustedly into the grass and looked back slightingly with other annihilating remarks close behind his wide-apart teeth, but instead of speaking he made an unbelievably quick motion with his hand. The blow smacked loudly upon Dunk's cheek, and so nearly sent him out of the saddle that he grabbed for the horn to save himself.

"Oh, I seert yuh keepin' yer hand next yer six-gun all the while," Big Medicine bawled. "That's one reason I say yuh ain't no man! Yuh wouldn't dast talk up to a prairie dog if yuh wasn't all set to make a quick draw. Yuh got your face slapped oncet before by a Flyin' U man, and yuh had it comm'. Now you're—gittin'—it—done—right!"

If you have ever seen an irate, proletarian mother cuffing her offspring over an empty wood-box, you may picture perhaps the present proceeding of Big Medicine. To many a man the thing would have been unfeasible, after the first blow, because of the horses. But Big Medicine was very nearly all that he claimed to be; and one of his pet vanities was his horsemanship; he managed to keep within a fine slapping distance of Dunk. He stopped when his hand began to sting through his glove.

"Now you keep your hand away from that gun—that you ain't honest enough to carry where folks can see it, but 'ye got it cached in your pocket!" he thundered. "And go on with what you was goin' t'say. Only don't get swell-headed enough to think you're a man, agin. You ain't."

"I've got this to say!" Mere type cannot reproduce the malevolence of Dunk's spluttering speech. "I've sent for the county sheriff and a dozen deputies to arrest you, and you, and you, damn you!" He was pointing a shaking finger at the older members of the Happy Family, whom he recognized not gladly, but too well. "I'll have you all in Deer Lodge before that lying, thieving, cattle-stealing Old Man of yours can lift a finger. I'll sheep Flying U coulee to the very doors of the white house. I'll skin the range between here and the river—and I'll have every one of you hounds put where the dogs won't bite you!" He drew a hand across his mouth and smiled as they say Satan himself can smile upon occasion.

"You've done enough to send you all over the road; destroying property and assaulting harmless men—you wait! There are other and better ways to fight than with the fists, and I haven't forgotten any of you fellows—there are a few more rounders among you—"

"Hey! You apologize fer that, by cripes, er I'll kill yuh the longest way I know. And that—" Big Medicine again laid violent hands upon Dunk, "and that way won't feel good, now I'm tellin' yuh. Apologize, er—"

"Say, all this don't do any good, Bud," Weary expostulated. "Let Dunk froth at the mouth if he wants to; what we want is to get these sheep off the range. And," he added recklessly, "so long as the sheriff is headed for us anyway, we may as well get busy and make it worth his while. So—" He stopped, silenced by a most amazing interruption.

On the brow of the hill, when first they had sighted Dunk in the hollow, something had gone wrong with Miguel's saddle so that he had stopped behind; and, to keep him company, Andy had stopped also and waited for him. Later, when Dunk was spluttering threats, they had galloped up to the edge of the group and pulled their horses to a stand. Now, Miguel rode abruptly close to Dunk as rides one with a purpose.

He leaned and peered intently into Dunk's distorted countenance until every man there, struck by his manner, was watching him curiously. Then he sat back in the saddle, straightened his legs in the stirrups and laughed. And like his smile when he would have it so, or the little twitch of shoulders by which he could so incense a man, that laugh brought a deeper flush to Dunk's face, reddened though it was by Big Medicine's vigorous slapping.

"Say, you've got nerve," drawled the Native Son, "to let a sheriff travel toward you. I can remember when you were more timid, amigo." He turned his head until his eyes fell upon Andy. "Say, Andy!" he called. "Come and take a look at this hombre. You'll have to think back a few years," he assisted laconically.

In response, Andy rode up eagerly. Like the Native Son, he leaned and peered into eyes that stared back defiantly, wavered, and turned away. Andy also sat back in the saddle then, and snorted.

"So this is the Dunk Whittaker that's been raising merry hell around here! And talks about sending for the sheriff, huh? I've always heard that a lot uh gall is the best disguise a man can hide under, but, by gracious, this beats the deuce!" He turned to the astounded Happy Family with growing excitement in his manner.

"Boys, we don't have to worry much about this gazabo! We'll just freeze onto him till the sheriff heaves in sight. Gee! There'll sure be something stirring when we tell him who this Dunk person really is! And you say he was in with the Old Man, once? Oh, Lord!" He looked with withering contempt at Dunk; and Dunk's glance flickered again and dropped, just as his hand dropped to the pocket of his coat.

"No, yuh don't, by cripes!" Big Medicine's hand gripped Dunk's arm on the instant. With his other he plucked the gun from Dunk's pocket, and released him as he would let go of something foul which he had been compelled to touch.

"He'll be good, or he'll lose his dinner quick," drawled the Native Son, drawing his own silver-mounted six-shooter and resting it upon the saddle horn so that it pointed straight at Dunk's diaphragm. "You take Weary off somewhere and tell him something about this deal, Andy. I'll watch this slippery gentleman." He smiled slowly and got an answering grin from Andy Green, who immediately rode a few rods away, with Weary and Pink close behind.

"Say, by golly, what's Dunk wanted fer?" Slim blurted inquisitively after a short silence.

"Not for riding or driving over a bridge faster than a walk Slim," purred the Native Son, shifting his gun a trifle as Dunk moved uneasily in the saddle. "You know the man. Look at his face—and use your imagination, if you've got any."

CHAPTER XIII. The Happy Family Learn Something

"Well, I hope this farce is about over," Dunk sneered, with as near an approach to his old, supercilious manner as he could command, when the three who had ridden apart returned presently. "Perhaps, Weary, you'll be good enough to have this fellow put up his gun, and these—" he hesitated, after a swift glance, to apply any epithet whatever to the Happy Family. "I have two witnesses here to swear that you have without any excuse assaulted and maligned and threatened me, and you may consider yourselves lucky if I do not insist—"

"Ah, cut that out," Andy advised wearily. "I don't know how it strikes the rest, but it sounds pretty sickening to me. Don't overlook the fact that two of us happen to know all about you; and we know just where to send word, to dig up a lot more identification. So bluffing ain't going to help you out, a darned bit."

"Miguel, you can go with Andy," Weary said with brisk decision. "Take Dunk down to the ranch till the sheriff gets here—if it's straight goods about Dunk sending for him. If he didn't, we can take Dunk in tomorrow, ourselves." He turned and fixed a cold, commanding eye upon the slack-jawed herders. "Come along, you two, and get these sheep headed outa here."

"Say, we'll just lock him up in the blacksmith shop, and come on back," Andy amended the order after his own free fashion. "He couldn't get out in a million years; not after I'm through staking him out to the anvil with a log-chain." He smiled maliciously into Dunk's fear-yellowed countenance, and waved him a signal to ride ahead, which Dunk did without a word of protest while the Happy Family looked on dazedly.

"What's it all about, Weary?" Irish asked, when the three were gone. "What is it they've got on Dunk? Must be something pretty fierce, the way he wilted down into the saddle."

"You'll have to wait and ask the boys." Weary rode off to hurry the herders on the far side of the band.

So the Happy Family remained perforce unenlightened upon the subject and for that they said hard things about Weary, and about Andy and Miguel as well. They believed that they were entitled to know the truth, and they called it a smart-aleck trick to keep the thing so almighty secret.

There is in resentment a crisis; when that crisis is reached, and the dam of repression gives way, the full flood does not always sweep down upon those who have provoked the disaster. Frequently it happens that perfectly innocent victims are made to suffer. The Happy Family had been extremely forbearing, as has been pointed out before. They had frequently come to the boiling point of rage and had cooled without committing any real act of violence. But that day had held a long series of petty annoyances; and here was a really important thing kept from them as if they were mere outsiders. When Weary was gone, Irish asked Pink what crime Dunk had committed in the past. And Pink shook his head and said he didn't know. Irish mentally accused Pink of lying, and his temper was none the better for the rebuff, as anyone can readily understand.

When the herders, therefore, rounded up the sheep and started them moving south, the Happy Family speedily rebelled against that shuffling, nibbling, desultory pace that had kept them long, weary hours in the saddle with the other band. But it was Irish who first took measures to accelerate that pace.

He got down his rope and whacked the loop viciously down across the nearest gray back. The sheep jumped, scuttled away a few paces and returned to its nibbling progress. Irish called it names and whacked another.

After a few minutes he grew tired of swinging his loop and seeing it have so fleeting an effect, and pulled his gun. He fired close to the heels of a yearling buck that had more than once stopped to look up at him foolishly and blat, and the buck charged ahead in a panic at the noise and the spat of the bullet behind him.

"Hit him agin in the same place!" yelled Big Medicine, and drew his own gun. The Happy Family, at that high tension where they were ready for anything, caught the infection and began shooting and yelling like crazy men.

The effect was not at all what they expected. Instead of adding impetus to the band, as would have been the case if they had been driving cattle, the result was exactly the opposite. The sheep ran—but they ran to a common center. As the shooting went on they bunched tighter and tighter, until it seemed as though those in the center must surely be crushed flat. From an ambling, feeding company of animals, they become a lumpy gray blanket, with here and there a long, vacuous face showing idiotically upon the surface.

The herders grinned and drew together as against a common enemy— or as with a new joke to be discussed among themselves. The dogs wandered helplessly about, yelped half-heartedly at the woolly mass, then sat down upon their haunches and lolled red tongues far out over their pointed little teeth, and tilted knowing heads at the Happy Family.

"Look at the darned things!" wailed Pink, riding twice around the huddle, almost ready to shed tears of pure rage and helplessness. "Git outa that! Hi! Woopp-ee!" He fired again and again, and gave the range-old cattle-yell; the yell which had sent many a tired herd over many a weary mile; the yell before which had fled fat steers into the stockyards at shipping time, and up the chutes into the cars; the yell that had hoarsened many a cowpuncher's voice and left him with a mere croak to curse his fate with; a yell to bring results—but it did not start those sheep.

The Happy Family, riding furiously round and round, fired every cartridge they had upon their persons; they said every improper thing they could remember or invent; they yelled until their eyes were starting from their sockets; they glued that band of sheep so tight together that dynamite could scarcely have pried them apart.

And the herders, sitting apart with grimy hands clasped loosely over hunched-up knees, looked on, and talked together in low tones, and grinned.

Irish glanced that way and caught them grinning; caught them pointing derisively, with heaving shoulders. He swore a great oath and made for them, calling aloud that he would knock those grins so far in that they would presently find themselves smiling wrong-side-out from the back of their heads.

Pink, overhearing him, gave a last swat at the waggling tail of a burrowing buck, and wheeled to overtake Irish and have a hand in reversing the grins. Big Medicine saw them start, and came bellowing up from the far side of the huddle like a bull challenging to combat from across a meadow. Big Medicine did not know what it was all about, but he scented battle, and that was sufficient. Cal Emmett and Weary, equally ignorant of the cause, started at a lope toward the trouble center.

It began to look as if the whole Family was about to fall upon those herders and rend them asunder with teeth and nails; so much so that the herders jumped up and ran like scared cottontails toward the rim of Denson coulee, a hundred yards or so to the west.

"Mamma! I wish we could make the sheep hit that gait and keep it," exclaimed Weary, with the first laugh they had heard from him that day.

While he was still laughing, there was a shot from the ridge toward which they were running; the sharp, vicious crack of a rifle. The Happy

Family heard the whistling hum of the bullet, singing low over their heads; quite low indeed; altogether too low to be funny. And they had squandered all their ammunition on the prairie sod, to hurry a band of sheep that flatly refused to hurry anywhere except under one another's odorous, perspiring bodies.

From the edge of the coulee the rifle spoke again. A tiny geyser of dust, spurting up from the ground ten feet to one side of Cal Emmett, showed them all where the bullet struck.

"Get outa range, everybody!" yelled Weary, and set the example by tilting his rowels against Glory's smooth hide, and heading eastward. "I like to be accommodating, all right, but I draw the line on standing around for a target while my neighbors practise shooting."

The Happy Family, having no other recourse, therefore retreated in haste toward the eastern skyline. Bullets followed them, overtook them as the shooter raised his sights for the increasing distance, and whined harmlessly over their heads. All save one.

CHAPTER XIV. Happy Jack

Big Medicine, Irish and Pink, racing almost abreast, heard a scream behind them and pulled up their horses with short, stiff-legged plunges. A brown horse overtook them; a brown horse, with Happy Jack clinging to the saddle-horn, his body swaying far over to one side. Even as he went hurtling past them his hold grew slack and he slumped, head foremost, to the ground. The brown horse gave a startled leap away from him and went on with empty stirrups flapping.

They sprang down and lifted him to a less awkward position, and Big Medicine pillowed the sweat-dampened, carroty head in the hollow of his arm. Those who had been in the lead looked back startled when the brown horse tore past them with that empty saddle; saw what had happened, wheeled and galloped back. They dismounted and stood silently grouped about poor, ungainly Happy Jack, lying there limp and motionless in Big Medicine's arms. Not one of them remembered then that there was a man with a rifle not more than two hundred yards away; or, if they did, they quite forgot that the rifle might be dangerous to themselves. They were thinking of Happy Jack.

Happy Jack, butt of all their jokes and jibes; Happy the croaker, the lugubrious forecaster of trouble; Happy Jack, the ugliest, the stupidest, the softest-hearted man of them all. He had "betched" there would be someone killed, over these Dot sheep; he had predicted trouble of every conceivable kind; and they had laughed at him, swore at him, lied to him, "joshed" him unmercifully, and kept him in a state of chronic indignation, never dreaming that the memory of it would choke them and strike them dumb with that horrible, dull weight in their chests with which men suffer when a woman would find the relief of weeping.

"Where's he hurt?" asked Weary, in the repressed tone which only tragedy can bring into a man's voice, and knelt beside Big Medicine.

"I dunno—through the lungs, I guess; my sleeve's gitting soppy right under his shoulder." Big Medicine did not bellow; his voice was as quiet as Weary's.

Weary looked up briefly at the circle of staring faces. "Pink, you pile onto Glory and go wire for a doctor. Try Havre first; you may get one up on the nine o' clock train. If you can't, get one down on the 'leven-twenty, from Great Falls. Or there's Benton—anyway, git one. If you could catch MacPherson, do it. Try him first, and never mind a Havre doctor unless you can't get MacPherson. I'd rather wait a couple of hours longer, for him. I'll have a rig—no, you better get a team from Jim. They'll be fresh, and you can put 'em through. If you kill 'em," he added grimly, "we can pay for 'em." He had his jack-knife out, and was already slashing carefully the shirt of Happy Jack, that he might inspect the wound.

Pink gave a last, wistful look at Happy Jack's face, which seemed unfamiliar with all the color and all the expression wiped out of it like that, and turned away. "Come and help me change saddles, Cal," he said shortly. "Weary's stirrups are too darned long." Even with the delay, he was mounted on Glory and galloping toward Flying U coulee before Weary was through uncovering the wound; and that does not mean that Weary was slow.

The rifle cracked again, and a bullet plucked into the sod twenty feet beyond the circle of men and horses. But no one looked up or gave any other sign of realization that they were still the target; they were staring, with that frowning painfully intent look men have at such moments, at a purplish hole not much bigger than if punched by a lead pencil, just under the point of Happy Jack's shoulder blade; and at the blood oozing sluggishly from it in a tiny stream across the girlishly white flesh and dripping upon Big Medicine's arm.

"Hadn't we better get a rig to take him home with?" Irish suggested.

Weary, exploring farther, had just disclosed a ragged wound under the arm where the bullet had passed out; he made no immediate reply.

"Well, he ain't got it stuck inside of 'im, anyway," Big Medicine commented relievedly. "Don't look to me like it's so awful bad—went through kinda anglin', and maybe missed his lungs. I've saw men shot up before—"

"Aw—I betche you'd—think it was bad—if you had it—" murmured Happy Jack peevishly, lifting his eyelids heavily for a resentful glance when they moved him a little. But even as Big Medicine grinned joyfully down at him he went off again into mental darkness, and the grin faded into solicitude.

"You'd kick, by golly, if you was goin' to be hung," Slim bantered tritely and belatedly, and gulped remorsefully when he saw that he was "joshing" an unconscious man.

"We better get him home. Irish, you—" Weary looked up and discovered that Irish and jack Bates were already headed for home and a conveyance. He gave a sigh of approval and turned his attention toward wiping the sweat and grime from Happy's face with his handkerchief.

"Somebody else is goin' to git hit, by golly, if we stay here," Slim blurted suddenly, when another bullet dug up the dirt in that vicinity.

"That gol-darned fool'll keep on till he kills somebody. I wisht I had m' thirty-thirty here—I'd make him wisht his mother was a man, by golly!"

Big Medicine looked toward the coulee rim. "I ain't got a shell left," he growled regretfully. "I wisht we'd thought to tell the boys to bring them rifles. Say, Slim, you crawl onto your hoss and go git 'em. It won't take more'n a minute. There'll likely be some shells in the magazines."

"Go on, Slim," urged Weary grimly. "We've got to do something. They can't do a thing like this—" he glanced down at Happy Jack— "and get away with it."

"I got half a box uh shells for my thirty-thirty, I'll bring that." Slim turned to go, stopped short and stared at the coulee rim. "By golly, they're comm' over here!" he exclaimed.

Big Medicine glanced up, took off his hat, crumpled it for a pillow and eased Happy Jack down upon it. He got up stiffly, wiped his fingers mechanically upon his trouser legs, broke his gun open just to make sure that it was indeed empty, put it back and picked up a handful of rocks.

"Let 'em come," he said viciously. "I c'n kill every damn' one with m' bare hands!"

CHAPTER XV. Oleson

"Say, ain't that Andy and Mig following along behind?" Cal asked after a minute of watching the approach. "Sure, it is. Now what—"

"They're drivin' 'em, by cripes!" Big Medicine, under the stress of the moment, returned to his usual bellowing tone. "Who's that tall, lanky feller in the lead? I don't call to mind ever seem him before. Them four herders I'd know a mile off."

"That?" Weary shaded his eyes with his hat-brim, against the slant rays of the westering sun. "That's Oleson, Dunk's partner."

"His mother'd be a-weepin'," Big Medicine observed bodefully, "if she knowed what was due to happen to her son right away quick. Must be him that done the shootin'."

They came on steadily, the four herders and Oleson walking reluctantly ahead, with Andy Green and the Native Son riding relentlessly in the rear, their guns held unwaveringly in a line with the backs of their captives. Andy was carrying a rifle, evidently taken from one of the men—Oleson, they judged for the guilty one. Half the distance was covered when Andy was seen to turn his head and speak briefly with the Native Son, after which he lunged past the captives and galloped up to the waiting group. His quick eye sought first the face of Happy Jack in anxious questioning; then, miserably, he searched the faces of his friends.

"Good Lord!" he exclaimed mechanically, dismounted and bent over the figure on the ground. For a long minute he knelt there; he laid his ear close to Happy Jack's mouth, took off his glove and laid his hand over Happy's heart; reached up, twitched off his neckerchief, shook out the creases and spread it reverently over Happy Jack's face. He stood up then and spoke slowly, his eyes fixed upon the stumbling approach of the captives.

"Pink told us Happy had been shot, so we rode around and come up behind 'em. It was a cinch. And—say, boys, we've got the Dots in a pocket. They've got to eat outa our hands, now. So don't think about— our own feelings, or about—" he stopped abruptly and let a downward glance finish the sentence. "We've got to keep our own hands clean, and—now don't let your fingers get the itch, Bud!" This, because of certain manifestations of a murderous intent on the part of Big Medicine.

"Oh, it's all right to talk, if yuh feel like talking," Big Medicine retorted savagely. "I don't." He made a catlike spring at the foremost man, who happened to be Oleson, and got a merciless grip with his fingers on his throat, snarling like a predatory animal over its kill. From behind, Andy, with Weary to help, pulled him off.

"I didn't mean to—to kill anybody," gasped Oleson, pasty white. "I heard a lot of shooting, and so I ran up the hill—and the herders came running toward me, and I thought I was defending my property and men. I had a right to defend—"

"Defend hell!" Big Medicine writhed in the restraining grasp of those who held him. "Look at that there! As good hearted a boy as ever turned a cow! Never harmed a soul in 'is life. Is all your dirty, stinkin' sheep, an' all your lousy herders, worth that boy's life? Yuh shot 'im down like a dog—lemme go, boys." His voice was husky. "Lemme tromp the life outa him."

"I thought you were killing my men, or I never—I never meant to—to kill—" Oleson, shaking till he could scarcely stand, broke down and wept; wept pitiably, hysterically, as men of a certain fiber will weep when black tragedy confronts them all unawares. He cowered miserably before the Happy Family, his face hidden behind his two hands.

"Boys, I want to say a word or two. Come over here." Andy's voice, quiet as ever, contrasted strangely with the man's sobbing. He led them back a few paces—Weary, Cal, Big Medicine and Slim, and spoke hurriedly. The Native Son eyed them sidelong from his horse, but he was careful to keep Oleson covered with his gun—and the herders too, although they were unarmed. Once or twice he glanced at that long, ungainly figure in the grass with the handkerchief of Andy Green hiding the face except where a corner, fluttering in the faint breeze which came creeping out of the west, lifted now and then and gave a glimpse of sunbrowned throat and a quiet chin and mouth.

"Quit that blubbering, Oleson, and listen here." Andys voice broke relentlessly upon the other's woe. "All these boys want to hang yuh without any red tape; far as I'm concerned, I'm dead willing. But we're going to give yuh a chance. Your partner, as we told yuh coming over, we've got the dead immortal cinch on, right now. And—well you can see what you're up against. But we'll give yuh a chance. Have you got any family?"

Oleson, trying to pull himself together, shook his head.

"Well, then, you can get rid of them sheep, can't yuh? Sell 'em, ship 'em outa here—we don't give a darn what yuh do, only so yuh get 'em off the range."

"Y-yes, I'll do that." Oleson's consent was reluctant, but it was fairly prompt. "I'll get rid of the sheep," he said, as if he was minded to clinch the promise. "I'll do it at once."

"That's nice." Andy spoke with grim irony. "And you'll get rid of the ranch, too. You'll sell it to the Flying U—cheap."

"But my partner—Whittaker might object—"

"Look here, old-timer. You'll fix that part up; you'll find a way of fixing it. Look here—at what you're up against." He waited, with pointing finger, for one terrible minute. "Will you sell to the Flying U?"

"Y-yes!" The word was really a gulp. He tried to avoid looking where Andy pointed; failed, and shuddered at what he saw.

"I thought you would. We'll get that in writing. And we're going to wait just exactly twenty-four hours before we make a move. It'll take some fine work, but we'll do it. Our boss, here, will fix up the business end with you. He'll go with yuh right now, and stay with yuh till you make good. And the first crooked move you make—" Andy, in unconscious imitation of the Native Son, shrugged a shoulder expressively and urged Weary by a glance to take the leadership.

"Irish, you come with me. The rest of you fellows know about what to do. Andy, I guess you'll have to ride point till I get back." Weary hesitated, looked from Happy Jack to Oleson and the herders, and back to the sober faces of his fellows. "Do what you can for him, boys—and I wish one of you would ride over, after Pink gets back, and—let me know how things stack up, will you?"

Incredible as was the situation on the face of it, nevertheless it was extremely matter-of-fact in the handling; which is the way sometimes with incredible situations; as if, since we know instinctively that we cannot rise unprepared to the bigness of its possibilities, we keep our feet planted steadfastly on the ground and refuse to rise at all. And afterward, perhaps, we look back and wonder how it all came about.

At the last moment Weary turned back and exchanged guns with Andy Green, because his own was empty and he realized the possible need of one—or at least the need of having the sheep-men perfectly aware that he had one ready for use. The Native Son, without a word of comment, handed his own silver-trimmed weapon over to Irish, and rolled a cigarette deftly with one hand while he watched them ride away.

"Does this strike anybody else as being pretty raw?" he inquired calmly, dismounting among them. "I'd do a good deal for the outfit, myself; but letting that man get off—Say, you fellows up this way don't think killing a man amounts to much, do you?" He looked from one to the other with a queer, contemptuous hostility in his eyes.

Andy Green took a forward step and laid a hand familiarly on his rigid shoulder. "Quit it, Mig. We would do a lot for the outfit; that's the God's truth. And I played the game right up to the hilt, I admit. But nobody's killed. I told Happy to play dead. By gracious, I caught him just in the nick uh time; he'd been setting up, in another minute." To prove it, he bent and twitched the handkerchief from the face of Happy Jack, and Happy opened his eyes and made shift to growl.

"Yuh purty near-smothered me t'death, darn yuh."

"Dios!" breathed the Native Son, for once since they knew him jolted out of his eternal calm. "God, but I'm glad!"

"I guess the rest of us ain't," insinuated Andy softly, and lifted his hat to wipe the sweat off his forehead. "I will say that—" After all, he did not. Instead, he knelt beside Happy Jack and painstakingly adjusted the crumpled hat a hair's breadth differently.

"How do yuh feel, old-timer?" he asked with a very thin disguise of cheerfulness upon the anxiety of his tone.

"Well, I could feel a lot—better, without hurtin' nothin," Happy Jack responded somberly. "I hope you fellers—feel better, now. Yuh got 'em—tryin' to murder—the hull outfit; jes' like I—told yuh they would—" Gunshot wounds, contrary to the tales of certain sentimentalists, do not appreciably sweeten, or even change, a man's disposition. Happy Jack with a bullet hole through one side of him was still Happy Jack.

"Aw, quit your beefin'," Big Medicine advised gruffly. "A feller with a hole in his lung yuh could throw a calf through sideways ain't got no business statin' his views on nothin', by cripes!"

"Aw gwan. I thought you said—it didn't amount t' nothin'," Happy reminded him, anxiety stealing into his face.

"Well, it don't. May lay yuh up a day or two; wouldn't be su'prised if yuh had to stay on the bed-ground two or three meals. But look at Slim, here. Shot through the leg—shattered a bone, by cripes!—las' night, only; and here he's makin' a hand and ridin' and cussin' same as any of us t'day. We ain't goin' to let yuh grouch around, that's all. We claim we got a vacation comm' to us; you're shot up, now, and that's fun enough for one man, without throwin' it into the whole bunch. Why, a little nick like that ain't nothin'; nothin' a-tall. Why, I've been shot right through here, by cripes"—Big Medicine laid an impressive finger-tip on the top button of his trousers—"and it come out back here"—he whirled and showed his thumb against the small of his back—"and I never laid off but that day and part uh the next. I was sore," he admitted, goggling Happy Jack earnestly, "but I kep' a-goin'. I was right in fall roundup, an' I had to. A man can't lay down an' cry, by cripes, jes' because he gets pinked a little—"

"Aw, that's jest because—it ain't you. I betche you'd lay 'em down—jest like other folks, if yuh got shot—through the lungs. That ain't no—joke, lemme tell yuh!" Happy Jack was beginning to show considerable spirit for a wounded man. So much spirit that Andy Green, who had seen men stricken down with various ills, read fever signs in the countenance and in the voice of Happy, and led Big Medicine somewhat peremptorily out of ear-shot.

"Ain't you got any sense?" he inquired with fine candor. "What do you want to throw it into him like that, for? You may not think so, but he's pretty bad off—if you ask me."

Big Medicine's pale eyes turned commiseratingly toward Happy Jack. "I know he is; I ain't no fool. I was jest tryin' to cheer 'im up a little. He was beginnin' to look like he was gittin' scared about it; I reckon maybe I made a break, sayin' what I did about it, so I jest wanted to take the cuss off. Honest to gran'ma—"

"If you know anything at all about such things, you must know what fever means in such a case. And, recollect, it's going to be quite a while before a doctor can get here."

"Oh, I'll be careful. Maybe I did throw it purty strong; I won't, no more." Big Medicine s meekness was not the least amazing incident of the day. He was a big-hearted soul under his bellow and bluff, and his sympathy for Happy Jack struck deep. He went back walking on his toes, and he stood so that his sturdy body shaded Happy Jack's face from the sun, and he did not open his mouth for another word until Irish and Jack Bates came rattling up with the spring wagon hurriedly transformed with mattress, pillows and blankets into an ambulance.

They had been thoughtful to a degree. They brought with them a jug of water and a tin cup, and they gave Happy Jack a long, cooling drink of it and bathed his face before they lifted him into the wagon. And of all the hands that ministered to his needs, the hands of Big Medicine were the eagerest and gentlest, and his voice was the most vibrant with sympathy; which was saying a good deal.

CHAPTER XVI. The End of the Dots

Slim may not have been more curious than his fellows, but he was perhaps more single-hearted in his loyalty to the outfit. To him the shooting of Happy Jack, once he felt assured that the wound was not necessarily fatal, became of secondary importance. It was all in behalf of the Flying U; and if the bullet which laid Happy Jack upon the ground was also the means of driving the hated Dots from that neighborhood, he felt, in his slow, phlegmatic way, that it wasn't such a catastrophe as some of the others seemed to think. Of course, he wouldn't want Happy to die; but he didn't believe, after all, that Happy was going to do anything like that. Old Patsy knew a lot about sickness and wounds.

106

(Who can cook for a cattle outfit, for twenty years and more, and not know a good deal of hurts?) Old Patsy had looked Happy over carefully, and had given a grin and a snort.

"Py cosh, dot vos lucky for you, alreatty," he had pronounced. "So you don't git plood-poisonings, mit fever, you be all right pretty soon. You go to shleep, yet. If fix you oop till der dochtor he cooms. I seen fellers shot plumb through der middle off dem, und git yell. You ain't shot so bad. You go to shleep."

So, his immediate fears relieved, Slim's slow mind had swung back to the Dots, and to Oleson, whom Weary was even now assisting to keep his promise (Slim grinned widely to himself when he thought of the abject fear which Oleson had displayed because of the murder he thought he had done, while Happy Jack obediently "played dead"). And of Dunk, whom Slim had hated most abominably of old; Dunk, a criminal found out; Dunk, a prisoner right there on the very ranch he had thought to despoil; Dunk, at that very moment locked in the blacksmith shop. Perhaps it was not curiosity alone which sent him down there; perhaps it was partly a desire to look upon Dunk humbled—he who had trodden so arrogantly upon the necks of those below him; so arrogantly that even Slim, the slow-witted one, had many a time trembled with anger at his tone.

Slim walked slowly, as was his wont; with deadly directness, as was his nature. The blacksmith shop was silent, closed—as grimly noncommittal as a vault. You might guess whatever you pleased about its inmate; it was like trying to imagine the emotions pictured upon the face behind a smooth, black mask. Slim stopped before the closed door and listened. The rusty, iron hasp attracted his slow gaze, at first puzzling him a little, making him vaguely aware that something about it did not quite harmonize with his mental attitude toward it. It took him a full minute to realize that he had expected to find the door locked, and that the hasp hung downward uselessly, just as it hung every day in the year.

He remembered then that Andy had spoken of chaining Dunk to the anvil. That would make it unnecessary to lock the door, of course. Slim seized the hanging strip of iron, gave it a jerk and bathed all the dingy interior with a soft, sunset glow. Cobwebs quivered at the inrush of the breeze, and glistened like threads of fine gold. The forge remained a dark blot in the corner. A new chisel, lying upon the earthen floor, became a bar of yellow light.

Slim's eyes went to the anvil and clung there in a widening stare. His hands, white and soft when his gloves were off, drew up convulsively into fighting fists, and as he stood looking, the cords swelled and stood out upon his thick neck. For years he had hated Dunk Whittaker—

The Happy Family, with rare good sense, had not hesitated to turn the white house into an impromptu hospital. They knew that if the Little Doctor and Chip and the Old Man had been at home Happy Jack would have been taken unquestioningly into the guest chamber—which was a square, three-windowed room off the big livingroom. More than one of them had occupied it upon occasion. They took Happy Jack up there and put him to bed quite as a matter-of-course, and when he was asleep they lingered upon the wide, front porch; the hammock of the Little Doctor squeaked under the weight of Andy Green, and the wide-armed chairs received the weary forms of divers young cowpunchers who did not give a thought to the intrusion, but were thankful for the comfort. Andy was swinging luxuriously and drawing the last few puffs from a cigarette when Slim, purple and puffing audibly, appeared portentously before him.

"I thought you said you was goin' to lock Dunk up in the blacksmith shop," he launched accusingly at Andy.

"We did," averred that young man, pushing his toe against the railing to accelerate the voluptuous motion of the hammock.

"He ain't there. He's broke loose. The chain—by golly, yuh went an' used that chain that was broke an' jest barely hangin' together! His horse ain't anywheres around, either. You fellers make me sick. Lollin' around here an' not paying no attention, by golly—he's liable to be ten mile from here by this time!" When Slim stopped, his jaw quivered like a dish of disturbed jelly, and I wish I could give you his tone; choppy, every sentence an accusation that should have made those fellows wince.

Irish, Big Medicine and Jack Bates had sprung guiltily to their feet and started down the steps. The drawling voice of the Native Son stopped them, ten feet from the porch.

"Twelve, or fifteen, I should make it. That horse of his looked to me like a drifter."

"Well—are yuh goin' t' set there on your haunches an' let him GO?" Slim, by the look of him, was ripe for murder.

"You want to look out, or you'll get apoplexy sure," Andy soothed, giving himself another luxurious push and pulling the last, little whiff from his cigarette before he threw away the stub. "Fat men can't afford to get as excited as skinny ones can."

"Aw, say! Where did you put him, Andy?" asked Big Medicine, his first flurry subsiding before the absolute calm of those two on the porch.

"In the blacksmith shop," said Andy, with a slurring accent on the first word that made the whole sentence perfectly maddening. "Ah, come on back here and sit down. I guess we better tell 'em the how of it. Huh, Mig?"

Miguel cast a slow, humorous glance over the four. "Ye-es— they'll have us treed in about two minutes if we don't," he assented. "Go ahead."

"Well," Andy lifted his head and shoulders that he might readjust a pillow to his liking, "we wanted him to make a getaway. Fact is, if he hadn't, we'd have been—strictly up against it. Right! If he hadn't—how about it, Mig? I guess we'd have been to the Little Rockies ourselves."

"You've got a sweet little voice," Irish cut in savagely, "but we're tired. We'd rather hear yuh say something!"

"Oh—all right. Well, Mig and I just ribbed up a josh on Dunk. I'd read somewhere about the same kinda deal, so it ain't original; I don't lay any claim to the idea at all; we just borrowed it. You see, it's like this: We figured that a man as mean as this Dunk person most likely had stepped over the line, somewhere. So we just took a gambling chance, and let him do the rest. You see, we never saw him before in our lives. All that identification stunt of ours was just a bluff. But the minute I shoved my chips to the center, I knew we had him dead to rights. You were there. You saw him wilt. By gracious—"

"Yuh don't know anything against him?" gasped Irish.

"Not a darned thing—any more than what you all know," testified Andy complacently.

It took a minute or two for that to sink in.

"Well, I'll be damned!" breathed Irish.

"We did chain him to the anvil," Andy went on. "On the way down, we talked about being in a hurry to get back to you fellows, and I told Mig—so Dunk could hear—that we wouldn't bother with the horse. We tied him to the corral. And I hunted around for that bum chain, and then we made out we couldn't find the padlock for the door; so we decided, right out loud, that he'd be dead safe for an hour or two, till the bunch of us got back. Not knowing a darn thing about him, except what you boys have told us, we sure would have been in bad if he hadn't taken a sneak. Fact is, we were kinda worried for fear he wouldn't have nerve enough to try it. We waited, up on the hill, till we saw him sneak down to the corral and jump on his horse and take off down the coulee like a scared coyote. It was," quoth the young man, unmistakably pleased with himself, "pretty smooth work, if you ask me."

"I'd hate to ride as fast and far to-night as that hombre will," supplemented Miguel with his brief smile, that was just a flash of white, even teeth and a momentary lightening of his languorous eyes.

Slim stood for five minutes, a stolid, stocky figure in the midst of a storm of congratulatory comment. They forgot all about Happy Jack, asleep inside the house, and so their voices were not hushed. Indeed, Big Medicine's bull-like remarks boomed full-throated across the coulee and were flung back mockingly by the barren hills. Slim did not hear a word they were saying; he was thinking it over, with that complete mental concentration which is the chief recompense of a slow-working mind. He was methodically thinking it all out—and, eventually, he saw the joke.

"Well, by golly!" he bawled suddenly, and brought his palm down with a terrific smack upon his sore leg—whereat his fellows laughed uproariously.

"We told you not to try to see through any more jokes till your leg gets well, Slim," Andy reminded condescendingly.

"Say, by golly, that's a good one on Dunk, ain't it? Chasin' himself clean outa the country, by golly—scared plumb to death—-and you fellers was only jest makin' b'lieve yuh knowed him! By golly, that sure is a good one, all right!"

"You've got it; give you time enough and you could see through a barbed-wire fence," patronized Andy, from the hammock. "Yes, since you mention it, I think myself it ain't so bad."

"Aw-w shut up, out there, an' let a feller sleep!" came a querulous voice from within. "I'd ruther bed down with a corral full uh calves at weanin' time, than be anywheres within ten mile uh you darned, mouthy—" The rest was indistinguishable, but it did not matter. The Happy Family, save Slim, who stayed to look after the patient, tiptoed penitently off the porch and took themselves and their enthusiasm down to the bunk-house.

CHAPTER XVII. Good News

Pink rolled over in his bed so that he might look—however sleepily—upon his fellows, dressing more or less quietly in the cool dawn-hour.

"Say, I got a letter for you, Weary," he yawned, stretching both arms above his head. "I opened it and read it; it was from Chip, so—"

"What did he have to say?"

"Old Man any better?"

"How they comm', back here?"

Several voices, speaking at once, necessitated a delayed reply.

"They'll be here, to-day or to-morrow," Pink replied without any circumlocution whatever, while he fumbled in his coat pocket for the letter. "He says the Old Man wants to come, and the doctors think he might as well tackle it as stay there fussing over it. They're coming in a special car, and we've got to rig up an outfit to meet him. The Little Doctor tells just how she wants things fixed. I thought maybe it was important—it come special delivery," Pink added naively, "so I just played it was mine and read it."

"That's all right, Cadwalloper," Weary assured him while he read hastily the letter. "Well, we'll fix up the spring wagon and take it in right away; somebody's got to go back anyway, with MacPherson. Hello, Cal; how's Happy?"

"All right," answered Cal, who had watched over him during the night and came in at that moment after someone to take his place in the sickroom. "Waked up on the fight because I just happened to be setting with my eyes shut. I wasn't asleep, but he said I was; claimed I snored so loud I kept him awake all night. Gee whiz! I'd ruther nurse a she bear with the mumps!"

"Old Man's coming home, Cal." Pink announced with more joy in his tone and in his face than had appeared in either for many a weary day. Whereupon Cal gave an exultant whoop. "Go tell that to Happy," he shouted. "Maybe he'll forget a grouch or two. Say, luck seems to be kinda casting loving glances our way again—what?"

"By golly, seems to me Pink oughta told us when he come in, las' night," grumbled Slim, when he could make himself heard.

"You were all dead to the world," Pink defended, "and I wanted to be. Two o'clock in the morning is a mighty poor time for elegant conversation, if you want my opinion."

"And the main point is, you knew all about it, and you didn't give a darn whether we did or not," Irish said bluntly. "And Weary sneaked in, too, and never let a yip outa him about things over in Denson coulee."

"Oh, what was the use?" asked Weary blandly. "I got an option out of Oleson for the ranch and outfit, and all his sheep, at a mighty good figure—for the Flying U. The Old Man can do what he likes about it; but ten to one he'll buy him out. That is, Oleson's share, which was two-thirds. I kinda counted on Dunk letting go easy. And," he added, reaching for his hat, "once I got the papers for it, there wasn't anything to hang around for, was there? Especially," he said with his old, sunny smile, "when we weren't urged a whole lot to stay."

Remained therefore little, save the actual arrival of the Old Man—a pitifully weak Old Man, bandaged and odorous with antiseptics, and quite pathetically glad to be back home—and his recovery, which was rather slow, and the recovery of Happy Jack, which was rapid.

For a brief space the Flying U outfit owned the Dots; very brief it was; not a day longer than it took Chip to find a buyer—at a figure considerably above that named in the option, by the way.

So, after a season of worry and trouble and impending tragedy such as no man may face unflinchingly, life dropped back to its usual level, and the trail of the Flying U outfit once more led through pleasant places.

End